EVIL LIVES HERE

A DCI JAMES CRAIG NOVEL

JOHN CARSON

DCI James Craig series
Ice Into Ashes
One of the Broken
Dead on Arrival
Whispers of Guilt
Evil Lives Here

DCI HARRY MCNEIL SERIES

Return to Evil
Sticks and Stones
Back to Life
Dead Before You Die
Hour of Need
Blood and Tears
Devil to Pay
Point of no Return
Rush to Judgement
Against the Clock
Fall from Grace
Crash and Burn
Dead and Buried
All or Nothing
Never go Home
Famous Last Words
Do Unto Others
Twist of Fate
Now or Never
Blunt Force Trauma

CALVIN STEWART SERIES
Final Warning
Hard Case

DCI SEAN BRACKEN SERIES
Starvation Lake
Think Twice
Crossing Over
Life Extinct
Over Kill

DI FRANK MILLER SERIES

Crash Point
Silent Marker
Rain Town
Watch Me Bleed
Broken Wheels
Sudden Death
Under the Knife
Trial and Error
Warning Sign
Cut Throat
Blood from a Stone
Time of Death
Old School - short story

Frank Miller Crime Series – Books 1-3 – Box set
Frank Miller Crime Series - Books 4-6 - Box set

MAX DOYLE SERIES
Final Steps
Code Red
The October Project

SCOTT MARSHALL SERIES

Old Habits

**EVIL LIVES HERE**

For the real Leanne Chalmers

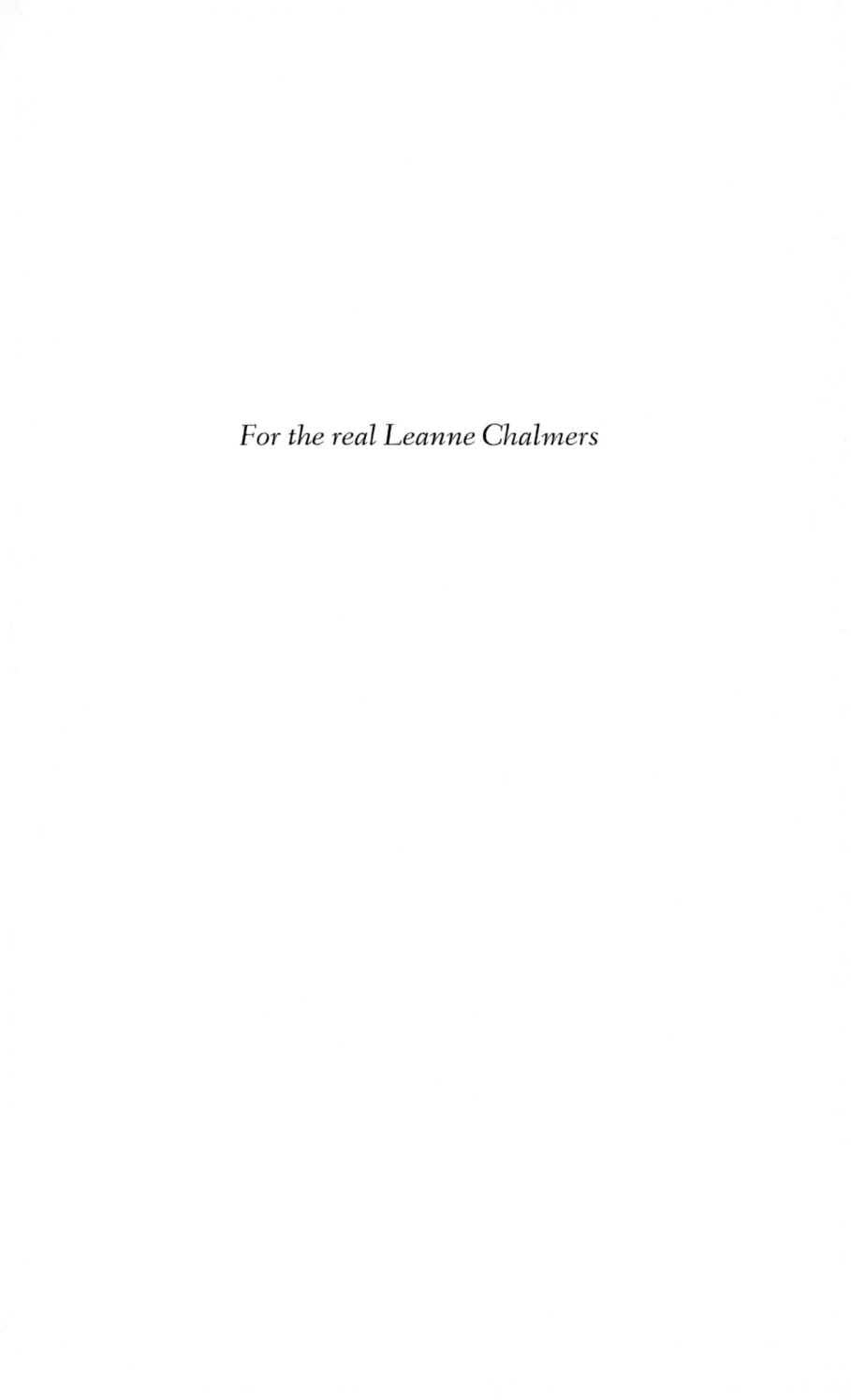

Copyright © 2025 John Carson

www.johncarsonauthor.com

John Carson has asserted his right under the Copyright, Designs and Patents Act 1988, to be identified as the author of this work.

This is a work of fiction. Names, characters, places, brands, media, and incidents are either the products of the author's imagination or are used fictitiously. Any resemblance to actual events, locales, or persons, living or dead, is coincidental.

Without limiting the rights under copyright reserved above, no part of this publication may be reproduced, stored in or introduced into a retrieval system, or transmitted, in any form, or by any means (electronic, mechanical, photocopying, recording, or otherwise) without the prior written permission of the author of this book. Innocence is and

All rights reserved

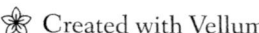 Created with Vellum

ONE

'You look like a half-shut knife,' Detective Sergeant Isla McGregor said, sitting down opposite her boss in the Tim Hortons on Hospital Hill in Dunfermline.

'You look like you're late.' Detective Chief Inspector James Craig looked at his watch before taking a sip from his coffee, sliding the other one across the table.

'The Uber driver was held up before he got to me,' Isla said. 'My car will be ready next Monday, they said.'

He yawned.

'Good God, I'd better not start yawning now. I've been up bright and early. Unlike yourself, clearly.' She smiled at him, looking at his unshaven face and eyes that were blue but bloodshot, before sipping at the hot coffee through the hole in the lid. Then she yawned.

'This was supposed to be our day off. Have a lie in, easy breakfast, take the dog to Heather's, head up to Inverness,' Craig said.

'Finn knows you're leaving him behind to go on a dirty weekend?'

'He's a dog.'

'So you lied to him, then?' Isla said.

'Of course I did. I still took him over anyway.' He rubbed a hand over his chin. 'I would have shaved later, but I got the phone call. So did Annie, and she was out of there before I was even dressed.'

'Story of my life.' She sipped, then looked her boss in the eye. 'Inverness? Was Spain just a wee bit out of your reach?'

'We're visiting an old friend of my dad's. Couple of nights away, relax, maybe catch a film at the cinema.' He drank some of his coffee. 'Are there any cinemas in Inverness?'

Isla shrugged. 'No idea. My dad used to call it going to the pictures.'

'I thought you knew everything.' Craig shook his head. 'I'll ask Annie if she wants to go to the pictures. See if she knows what I'm havering about.'

'You do that. She'll understand. Because you're older than her.'

'Only by a couple of years. But she's more educated than I am. I'm sure she'll get it.'

'I'm sure she will, if you're going away for the weekend.'

Craig made a face. 'It's too early for this.' He stood up and Isla followed suit. He reached into his pocket and tossed her his car key fob. She caught it one-handed. 'Here, you can drive.'

'Feeling buzzed?'

'A little bit. I didn't have to drive too far to get here,' Craig said, grabbing his coffee cup.

Isla grabbed hers too. 'I could have got the Uber to Annie's house.'

'If I hadn't got up when I called you, I never would have got up. It was easier this way. Besides, I can snooze on the way. Just a little power nap. I checked Google; it's half an hour away. Plenty of time to get my feet up. As it were.'

Isla looked over at the counter. 'Would it be bad if I had a doughnut this early in the morning?'

'Don't ask me. I skipped breakfast this morning.'

'Couldn't open the plastic bag in the cereal box again?'

Craig nodded. 'I got there in the end. Bag

exploded. Cereal scattered all over the kitchen floor. Turns out Finn likes cornflakes after all. Who knew?'

Isla stopped Craig's Volvo behind a marked patrol car and Craig woke up. 'Just resting my eyes,' he said.

'Fake snoring too? A man of many hidden talents.'

Craig looked out at the old hotel. The ground-floor windows had been boarded up, and some of the upper windows had been smashed, but it was the roof that caught his eye. Or lack of it. Only blackened timbers remained, some pointing at him like accusing fingers.

He ran a hand over his face, then stretched his shoulders back. His eyes were tired and he felt like he had no energy, despite the caffeine intake, which in some parts of the world might have killed a mule. He had spent the night at his girlfriend's house, and he'd had to remind himself that he was forty-seven, not twenty-seven anymore. Maybe in his mind he was, but his body begged to differ.

They stepped out into the cold, taking the two disposable cups of coffee with them. Isla peeled off and approached a uniform.

'Morning, sir,' a young female said, walking across to Craig. DC Jessie Bell.

'Morning. What have we got going on here?' He sipped the coffee, which had turned cold.

'Two victims upstairs,' she said, turning to look at the hotel. 'This is a weird one, boss; I'll let you see for yourself rather than try and explain it.'

'You know I don't like surprises.'

'My words couldn't describe the scene adequately.'

'Okay then. Is Annie up there?'

'Yes, she is. She's just as dumbfounded, but used a different vocabulary to describe the scene.'

'Like what?'

'You know her just as well as I do, sir. The F-word was bandied about.'

Craig nodded, knowing all too well what Annie could be like at a crime scene.

'I spoke to one of the uniforms from Cupar,' Isla said, coming back over, 'and he was here the night the hotel went on fire three years ago.'

'Arson?' Craig said, walking towards the front of the hotel, which was surrounded by wire fencing panels sitting in concrete blocks.

Isla sipped her coffee and shook her head. 'Technically, yes, but the teenager they found here said that he and his friends just started the fire to keep warm. They were here smoking weed. Then the fire got out of control. There were three of them, but he fell down the stairs and broke his leg. There was no sign of the others when the patrol turned up. He didn't give up the names of the others. He got sent down for two years.'

'Do we have his name?' Craig asked.

'Christopher Gregory. Released two months ago.'

'I'll get Max to look him up,' Craig said. DI Max Hold, one of Craig's team. 'Can you deal with that, Jessie?'

'Yes, sir,' she said, walking away and taking her phone out.

'Are you all still having a drink with Jessie tonight, since it's her last day working with us?' Craig asked.

Isla nodded. 'The golf club in Dunfermline.'

'I thought Jessie lived in Leven?'

'She does. She's going to crash at my place tonight.'

'I might come along since my dirty weekend was blown out of the water. I'll bring the sweary one.' Sweary one; his nickname for Annie. She wasn't exactly Mary Poppins but knew how to rein it in, in a social situation.

'The more the merrier.' Isla smiled and got back to talking about their crime scene. 'The fire brigade managed to contain the fire to the top level,' she said, 'but it suffered severe damage, and the hotel had to close until repairs were made. Said repairs are still waiting for the go-ahead.'

'Insurance company not playing ball, I assume,' Craig said.

'If they are, the wheels are turning slowly. But nobody's been in here since that night. Not workers, anyway. There was a report of vandalism by one of the residents from those houses there.' She pointed to two cottages on the other side of the T-junction. 'The hotel has been boarded up since the fire, and the little terraced houses there. They were rentals, owned by the same guy who owns the hotel.'

Craig looked at the wire fencing panels sitting in concrete blocks. Two of them were displaced at the entrance to the hotel. 'Were they like that when uniforms arrived?'

Isla sipped her coffee, made a face and nodded. 'Yes. The panels were put in place after the vandalism episode.'

'Who made the call today?'

'A bus driver doing his last run last night, just after midnight. He stopped at the bus stop there, outside the terraced houses. He was running a bit early so he stopped there, then had a cigarette. He said he saw torchlight at one of the windows on the first floor, so he called us. Uniforms came out and found the fence had been moved. Then they went in and found the victims.'

Craig nodded and drank more coffee. 'Stan and his crew been in?'

'Yes. They've done their videoing and photography and they're trawling all over the building.'

'Is it safe in there?'

'The back annexe took the brunt of the fire, and an engineer came out and chatted with the fire brigade, and said the front part here is safe, but not to go near the back. The engineer wasn't happy about letting us in, but considering what was waiting for us, he had no option.'

Craig saw Stan Mackay, head of forensics, walk up to the back of his van. 'Where's Dan?' he asked Isla. DS Dan Stevenson, one of Craig's team.

'He's coming now. He was over with a couple of uniforms at those wee cottages, seeing if anybody heard or saw anything.'

'Right. Let's go and talk to Stan.'

They walked up behind Stan, who was peering into the van at something they couldn't see.

'Stan, how you doing, my friend?' Craig said.

Mackay spun around. 'Jesus, Jimmy. I nearly shat myself. You know, it's a medical fact that every time you get a fright, five minutes gets knocked off your life.'

'I thought that was cigarettes?'

'Those too. We should probably throw doughnuts into the mix as well. Just don't tell Dan.'

Dan walked up behind Craig. 'Don't tell Dan what?'

Craig looked at him. 'Stan doesn't think you have long to live.'

'What? Pish. I'm in my prime.'

Stan raised his eyebrows and shared a knowing look with Craig.

'What have you heard?' Dan said.

'Don't worry about it, Dan. Let's just say we'll skip Tim Hortons at lunchtime,' Craig said, raising his cup with Tim Hortons written on the side just to show that whatever ailment Dan had, it wasn't catching.

Stan grinned.

'What are we looking at in here, Stan?' Craig asked.

'Go and see for yourself.'

'That's both you and Jessie telling me to go and

have a look. Is it like the St Valentine's Day massacre?'

Stan shook his head. 'It's just weird. Tell him, Dan.'

Dan looked at Craig. 'Weird. Annie's in there with the latest guests, both of whom are well dead. Be careful, it's a bloody minefield.'

Craig looked at Isla and Dan. 'Have a word with the uniforms. See if they had any other reports about people entering in here.'

'Okay, boss.'

They both walked away, and Craig walked through the gap in the wire fence to the doorway, where a box of plastic shoe protectors sat.

'You'd better slip those on,' said Stan, who had followed him. 'Not for cross-contamination; more like you'd have to bin your boots after this, the place is so manky.'

Craig slipped a pair on and entered the building. Some battery lamps lit the interior. 'Am I going upstairs?' he asked Stan.

'Aye. I'm surprised. If the polis turned up, he would have had a better chance of nicking out the back. But for some reason he chose to work up there.'

'Less chance of anybody spotting him right away,' Craig answered.

'True. You know, this was a nice place. I came to the restaurant with the wife a while back. It'll be worth somebody sinking a few notes into the building, bring it back to life. It seems solid enough.' Stan nodded towards the front door. 'First floor, second door on your right. Have fun.' He turned and walked away, leaving the hotel again.

Craig didn't know if the man was suggesting he go upstairs and get it on with Annie or not, but he turned and walked inside the courtyard in front of the hotel. A couple of picnic benches sat abandoned, having seen better days. The weather had taken its toll on them as they waited for patrons to come back.

Inside, the building smelled of decay and smoke. The air smelled of mould and damp, with a hint of burnt wood. The pattern on the carpet was barely recognisable, covered in dirt and debris. The walls were grubby and a print of a man sitting on a horse in the countryside was askew on the left.

He climbed the stairs, the carpet throwing up little dust clouds as he stomped his feet. He reached the first landing and went into a large bedroom.

'Morning again,' he said to Annie, who had her back to him.

She spun round. 'Jesus,' the white-suited woman

yelled at him. His girlfriend, pathologist Annie Keller.

'As fake orgasms go, that's not your best one.'

Annie shook her head. 'There's nothing fake about me. Including the mini heart attack you just gave me.'

He grinned and looked around him. The room would have been lucky to get a one-star review on Tripadvisor, depending on how fussy you were. A double bed sat against one wall, the covers looking like burnt skin that had peeled. Something vaguely resembling a pillow sat against one wall. Curtains, covered in filth and hanging at an angle that would bring tears to an interior designer, were pulled apart, revealing windows that hadn't seen water on the inside in a very long time. The carpet was threadbare and covered in what Craig thought might be waste from a nuclear spill. Or certainly from a bin bag. The smell hit his nostrils in here, a familiar but not welcome smell that he'd first encountered when he had been in uniform.

But it was the tableau in front of him that grabbed his attention.

'I hope when you take me away for the weekend, it's a better hotel than this,' she said.

'I can't promise anything.' He looked at the two

victims, one female and the other male. The woman was sitting in an armchair, very much dead. Her face was deathly pale, her cheeks were sunken in and her eyes were closed. So were her lips, like she was grimacing, and her head was hanging to one side. On the floor at her feet, in front of a small fireplace, was the man, who was wearing a white vest, trousers and black shoes. Nothing else. The vest was covered in what Craig assumed were stab marks, blood covering the material, thicker in some places than others.

'Both dead, the female obviously for a lot longer than the male,' Craig said. 'She's dressed in a nice dress; he's wearing a vest and manky trousers. Scruffy bastard. Why were they up here together?' He looked at Annie. 'You don't think it was a Halloween prank gone wrong, do you?'

'You're the detective, sweetheart. I just solve puzzles of the cadaver kind.'

Craig turned round as he heard more feet shuffling outside the room. Detective Superintendent Mark Baker poked his head round the doorway.

'Talking of scruffy bastards, here's Mark,' Annie said. 'Why don't you come in instead of skulking about out there? You're making the place look untidy.' She stood with her hands on her hips as Baker entered the room.

'I don't want to trip and ruin my new suit,' Baker said.

'Decided to splash out on some new threads? Not before time.' She tutted at him. 'Don't tell me you've met somebody else already?'

Baker entered the room, and took a cotton hanky out of his pocket and put it up to his nose, ignoring the question.

'You have been to a crime scene before,' Annie said.

'I know. It's honking in here,' Baker said, looking at the two victims.

'Did you pass out when you were a probationer attending a postmortem?'

He looked at her, searching her face to see if she knew the answer. 'Of course not. What do we have here?'

'Liar.' Annie's suit rustled as she moved about, pointing to the bodies. 'I've examined them both,' she said. 'The man on the floor was Richard Goode, according to his driving licence.'

Baker looked at Craig, who nodded slightly.

'What's going on?' Annie asked.

'Jimmy here recognises the name. Just like I do. He was before your time. Goode was one of us,' Baker said.

'When you say, one of you...?' Annie said.

'I don't mean the travelling circus. Back then he was known as PC Richard Goode, many moons ago. Before he got invited to leave. You remember that, Jimmy?'

'I do,' Craig confirmed. 'I wasn't long in uniform. Goode as a Man Short, they called him. The other uniforms thought he was a useless bastard.'

'Dare I ask why?' Annie said, looking down at the dead man, then back up at Baker.

The DSup hesitated for a moment.

Craig jumped in. 'He and his partner got set about by a group of thugs, and Goode's partner was stabbed and got his jaw broken. Goode said he got taken round the corner and had to fight off another attacker, but there was no sign of anybody else. And he looked remarkably unscathed compared to his partner.'

Baker nodded. 'There was an investigation and Goode was cleared of any wrongdoing. There were other times when he was, how shall we say, not there to back up his partner. He was a coward. After that, nobody wanted to work with him. He resigned.'

'Jesus,' Annie said. 'Poor guy.' She looked at Craig. 'This puzzled Stan and me: the burnt newspapers over there in the corner.'

'What about them?' Craig answered.

'Stan said it looked like the papers were set on fire and then put out with the fire extinguisher. It's fresh, not part of the original fire.'

Craig walked over to the blackened papers. Some of them weren't burnt. He knelt down and looked at the top of the newspaper and saw it was part of a *Dunfermline Press*, dated the day before. 'Was this the killer? It would be a coincidence if it wasn't,' he said, answering his own question.

'Maybe he was cold,' Baker said.

Craig looked at him. 'All due respect, sir, the roof is mostly off. I don't think setting fire to a newspaper was going to help much.'

'Maybe he wasn't happy with the football scores.' Baker shrugged.

'Do they have football scores in Wednesday's paper?' Annie said, her eyebrows raised and using a voice that she might use with a five-year-old.

'I'm just throwing that out there. I couldn't tell you what's in the paper as I get all my news online.' Baker looked at her, waiting for the challenge, but none came.

'I don't follow the football anyway,' Annie said. Case closed.

Craig looked at them both, then brought the

conversation back to the crime scene. 'That wasn't a big enough fire to keep him warm. And why put it out again?'

'Maybe he had started it, but then a car stopped outside,' Baker suggested. 'He had to put it out in a hurry.'

'Maybe,' Craig conceded.

'It's looking like one of the stab wounds could have gone into his heart,' Annie said, 'but I'll make a definitive finding when I get him on my table.'

'What about the female?' Craig asked.

Annie smiled, but there was no humour in it. 'This is one sick bastard we're dealing with, Jim. She's been dead a long time. Not sure how long, but watch this.' Annie walked quietly over to the female and opened the woman's shirt, revealing breasts that were intersected by a Y-incision. Then she turned back to look at both men.

'She's already had a postmortem. A long time ago. Whoever she is, she was dead and buried. Then brought back up out of the ground. He dug her up out of her grave.'

TWO

London

'What do you think?' Mary Sturgeon said to her husband. They were in the living room in their private quarters in the small hotel. She pointed up to the ceiling with a spatula.

Brian Sturgeon looked up at the crack that had appeared in the plaster a few months back. He had given many a thought to fixing it, but it was easier to sit and ignore it. Maybe if the ceiling caved in he'd have a go. Mary said they'd be lucky if they weren't killed in their bed when the whole building came down. 'It's a small crack,' Brian said. 'Easy fix. Nothing to worry about.' Although the thought of their bedroom floor giving way and Mary crashing down on top of him had at least caused him to look at a DIY video on YouTube to see what stuff he'd need to buy to make the repairs. One day he might even get in the car and drive to the store to purchase said items.

'I told you I'd get round to it at the weekend,' Brian said, tutting at her, asserting his position of top of the household.

'You said that months ago.' Mary imagined the spatula taking an eye out, preferably one of Brian's. Give him something to think about. Or maybe her own, so she wouldn't have to stand at the cooker all day, although young Petra, the woman who came in to help, was a godsend, bless her.

'And I'm saying it again,' Brian said, picking up his newspaper and holding it up to his face.

'And we do the dance once more. But that wasn't really my point; it was that weirdo up on the second floor banging his door that made me think that he's contributed to the crack. Look at it; it's grown at least a foot since last Saturday when he first banged his door.'

Mary shook her head and looked up at the ceiling again. She's told her latest guest not to slam the door and shake the whole building. He'd smiled that guffy smile of his and apologised. His teeth would keep a dentist in enough work to at least put a deposit down on a new boat. They weren't quite at the amber traffic light colour yet, but they were definitely close to being the same shade as the magnolia paint they had slapped on every wall in the guest rooms. Brian knew a man who could get anything and who boasted he could nick anything if it wasn't nailed down. The fact that the large cans of paint had turned up with paint round the edges and not full was overlooked because they were a bargain. Maybe the friend could get his hands on some cheap plaster, or whatever it was that could repair the ceiling.

'He's a paying guest, and has given us the money on time, every time,' Brian said from behind his paper. God knew he loved his wife, but she was dyslexic, and when she had first seen his name written down, she'd thought he was a brain surgeon. It had taken a couple of goes to get it through to her that he wasn't that talented and his name was Brian Sturgeon.

The man with a penchant for testing out the hinges on the door to his room was called Harvey, and Mary had thought that *Hairy* was a funny name for a bloke, until he had explained. But what she lacked in reading skills she more than made up for in verbal sparring prowess, and she would have gone upstairs and kicked Harvey out in a heartbeat if Brian slipped her off the leash. But that would decrease their revenue, and they couldn't afford to lose another guest.

They'd lost a female guest a few months ago because she had 'looked at Brian funny' and laughed a little too long and hard at his jokes. Mary's jealousy was just another thorn in his side.

He'd had a few chats with Harvey, who seemed like a decent bloke. He even threw a few extra quid their way because he worked in his room. Something to do with computers, he'd told Brian. Working remotely, he added. So he would be spending a lot of time in there.

Mary had worried about the man, hoping he wasn't a drug dealer or something. Brian had reminded his wife that drug dealers tended to go about in black BMWs and dressed a lot more smartly than Harvey.

'It could be a disguise,' Mary had said.

'If it is, it's a bloody good one: holes in his cardy, shoes that look like they've been fished out of a skip, and facial hair that would give an ape a run for its money. Aye, he's working for a cartel right enough.'

Brian had shaken his head and gone about his business. His wife watched too much TV, that was her problem.

'Well, when you see him, remind him not to bang the room door.'

'Why don't I suggest he leave his laptop open while I'm at it? So you can have a better look, instead of trying to guess his password. You know, when you go in to clean his room.'

'That's a terrible thing to say. I was only moving it that time you saw me in there standing next to it.'

'Whatever keeps you off the ledge.'

'Anyway, dinner's almost ready. One last look around the dining room if you don't mind.'

Brian made a noise like he was trying to clear his throat and put the paper down before getting up out of his chair. 'Fine. But I'm not going to bug Harvey while he's eating dinner.'

Mary walked back through to the large kitchen, spatula swinging in her hand. Besides, she didn't have to guess the man's password. He'd left a little notebook lying about in his sock drawer.

UNTITLED

Harvey stood looking out of the window of his guest room at the new building opposite. Waiting and watching, his binoculars on the windowsill in front of him. The small pair he had bought to replace the large ones that had felt like he was wearing a scaled-down version of the Hubble telescope.

'Bird watching,' he'd told the nosey old bastard from downstairs. She'd knocked on his door and brought his laundry in one day, catching him looking out of the window and giving him a look like she'd just caught him with his trousers around his ankles.

'See any tits out there?' Mary had said.

'I beg your pardon?' Harvey had said, ready to

splutter and protest loudly that what he was doing was a countrywide hobby, but then she had nodded to the binoculars in his hand. He had told the landlady his name was Harvey. Had showed his fake ID, and she and her husband had smiled and taken his money.

'Birds,' she said. 'That *is* what you told my husband you're into, isn't it? Blue tits, robins and pigeons. That sort of thing.'

'Oh, yes. Birds. Of course.'

They'd stood there facing each other, like a verbal sparring was about to start and she had the upper hand, but then she'd nodded to the laundry basket she was holding with some of his shirts in it. Despite her thinking that he shopped at Le Garbage Can for his clothes, the shirts were new and of decent quality. Same with his underwear. Marks and Sparks. He must have been sentimentally attached to the holey jumper then. Hoarding bastard.

'Oh, right, sorry. Let me get that.'

She handed over the basket. 'Bring it downstairs when you're done with it. Like, this evening. I have more to do.'

'Have it now,' he had told her, gently tipping the clothes onto his bed. Mary was a dab hand with a washing machine (although it was hardly going down to the river and banging his shirts with rocks), and was an absolute master with the iron. If it was up to him, he'd burn the lot once a week and start afresh every weekend. Lazy arsehole, his old mum had said, but he preferred to call it being domestically challenged. He was sure that was a disability nowadays.

'Thanks,' Mary had said.

He had stood, waiting for her to retreat with the plastic laundry basket, and she had closed the door gently. She had reminded him before not to slam the door, and he'd reminded her that by law his door should have a working automatic fire door closer. She had assured him that her husband would get right on it, but he'd said he wouldn't tell if she didn't. The Mexican standoff was hovering between them, and he'd banged the door more than once just to piss her off.

Now, he was looking through the small binoculars, which could be slipped into a pocket when he was out. He also carried a little book of ornithology with him, in case some bothersome copper asked him to turn his pockets out. And Harvey had actually read through some of it, gleaning what information he needed to make himself look like if not an expert then certainly an enthusiastic amateur. Whether he could actually tell the difference between a pigeon and a seagull was borderline.

As he'd stood at the window with the lights off and only the nets for cover, darkness had fallen outside, making his job a little more difficult. In daylight, he could pick out the car approaching, no problem, but now the orange glow from the streetlights distorted the light and all he could see were headlights coming. Not all of the vehicles were going to be turning into the building opposite, though.

He had plenty of time to watch. Nowhere else to go, nothing else to do, except wait and watch.

Something he was used to doing.

THREE

Craig was halfway out of his car when his phone rang. He fumbled around in his pocket for it, digging past a comb, a packet of mints and his keys before finding the thing.

Isla locked the car and indicated that she would see him inside. He nodded to her.

It was Eve, his estranged wife. *Fuck*. He held the phone in his hand like it was a grenade with the pin out. Should he answer it? Listen to her moaning or berating him again? Or was it just another drunken rambling? Answer it or not? He saw the time; at least it wasn't Saturday night and she was two bottles in.

'Hello,' he said, the wind whipping across the car park. If he wore his hair longer, it would have been up and dancing, and if it was a wig, forget about it.

As it was, he had no fear of his close-cropped hair blowing anywhere.

'Jimmy, it's me,' Eve said.

'I know it is.' He tried to keep the bitterness out of his voice but felt it creeping in there, like a bad taste. His wife had left him to go and live near the State Hospital in Carstairs, and she'd wanted him to jack in his job and move with her. 'And do what?' he'd asked her. She didn't have the answer, and he had refused. Then she'd given him an ultimatum: 'move down there, or I'm calling it a day'.

Their son was incarcerated in the hospital at the time, so Craig knew it would be impossible to change her mind about the move, but he had tried. God knew he had tried. But then his son had been murdered in the hospital, and Eve had come back to Fife.

'I was wondering if we could talk?' Eve said, a slight edge of desperation in her voice.

Craig would be lying if he said he didn't feel sorry for his wife, and if he was honest with himself, he couldn't hate her. Did he still have feelings for her? Yes, undeniably. He'd known her for a very long time. Would he consider rekindling their marriage? No. This wasn't the first time she'd kicked him into touch. There would be no third time.

'When were you thinking? I'm about to head into the station.' He started walking towards the building. A drab affair that wouldn't have looked out of place on a housing estate built a long time ago.

'This afternoon, if you aren't busy.'

The wind tried snatching him away from the conversation, but he fought it, thinking about the hot mug of coffee that would soon be his.

'I think that would be fine,' he replied.

'If your girlfriend is okay with that.' There was some bitterness in her voice, but he could tell she was reining it in. After all, she'd been sleeping with a doctor from the State Hospital.

'What time?' he asked, not wanting to be drawn into an argument.

'I was thinking about four.'

'We just caught a case, so I'm not sure if I can make that. I'll play it by ear and let you know.'

'I understand,' Eve said.

'Whereabouts?' he asked, then knew by her hesitation what she wanted.

'I'd like to see Finn.' Their German Shepherd.

'Do you think that's a good idea? He'll think you've just been away somewhere, then he'll wonder where you've gone again.'

'I miss him, Jimmy.'

You shouldn't have fucking left him, then.

'It's not a good idea. You told me I could keep him and you wouldn't fight me on it. That means not letting him see you.' *I tell him you're dead,* he wanted to say, but kept it to himself.

'Fine. How about a coffee somewhere?'

'Kirkcaldy Galleries. They have a nice wee café.'

'Okay, Jimmy. See you there at four, unless you tell me otherwise.'

Craig stood just outside the entrance doors to HQ, thoughts running through his head. He wondered what line he should take to end the call: pleasant, formal or somewhere in between? She clicked off at his silence, making him feel like a heavy breather.

'Fuck it,' he said, walking in.

The other members of his team were busy upstairs in the incident room. Now that DC Jessie Bell was leaving, they would be even busier.

Craig took his overcoat off and hung it on the coat stand. He looked over at DS Gary Menzies. 'Any chance that kettle might turn itself on? With your help, of course.'

'Right on it, boss.' Gary got up from his desk and walked over to the kettle and poured some more bottled water into it to top it up. 'Anybody else?'

'Aye, maybe I'll have another,' DI Max Hold said, holding out his mug. 'There's a wee bit of dregs in there, but it doesn't matter. Just fill her up, pal.'

Menzies grabbed the mug.

'Not for me,' DS Dan Stevenson said. 'This cold weather and too much caffeine play havoc with my bladder.'

'You're fifty, Dan, not sixty,' Craig said.

'You're only three years away from my age. It's coming for you.'

'Just as well I've got a bladder like an iron boiler.'

'Mark my words,' Dan said, sitting down at his desk.

Isla walked over to the table where they kept their coffee paraphernalia. 'I'll have one, Gary. Your coffee is a close second to Tim Hortons'.'

'Flattery will get you everywhere. But you just want me to buy you drink at tonight's do, don't you?'

'Don't be silly. But if you insist. The boss is coming now that his weekend away with Annie has been ruined.'

'Maybe we could get him to let his wallet see the light of day.'

'I heard that, Menzies,' Craig said.

'Just me jesting, sir,' Gary replied, watching the kettle to see if it would boil faster. No such luck.

Craig walked over to the whiteboard, where Jessie was sticking up notes. There was a photo of Richard Goode up there.

Jessie turned to look at him. 'I got this from HR. It's an old one, but it'll do for visual purposes.'

'Good job.' He turned to face the others. 'Let's get started on this.'

Gary handed him his mug of coffee.

'Cheers, son.' Craig took a sip and it nearly burnt his lip off. He put the mug down on a side table and looked at the faces turned to him.

'We were at the old, ruined hotel this morning. Apparently, once upon a time it was a nice wee place for the outdoorsy types. Hiking, fishing, that sort of stuff. It caught fire three years ago.' He turned to Max, who had also joined the burnt lip club. They really needed to tell Gary to add more milk when he was making the drinks. 'Did you find out about Christopher Gregory? The guy who was caught for arson at the hotel.'

Max nodded. 'Aye. He's out now. I got an address for him. I figured you would want to go round personally and have a talk with him.'

'I do. I'm holding him personally responsible for buggering my weekend off.'

'How so, sir?' Gary asked.

'I'm in here, answering your question, instead of being up north.'

'That would make me cranky as well,' Gary said, nodding.

'As well as who?' Craig said.

Gary at least had the grace to pull a beamer. 'Just somebody else I know.'

'Right.' Craig looked at Max. 'What else do we have on the hotel?'

'Owned by the Renaissance Hotel Group, based in London. They've been buying up properties in Scotland, including a few in Edinburgh and Glasgow, and one in Inverness. Bars too. That was the first one that wasn't in a city.'

Craig nodded and had another go at the coffee, hoping that he wouldn't need plastic surgery on his lips this time. He gave a good blow across the surface to try to chase away some of the heat. Better, but the first burn still smarted. 'Isla, you said the hotel's been burnt out for three years.'

'Yes, sir.'

'Find out what the delay in fixing it back up is. If the insurance company really are dragging their heels, and if they are, I want to know why.'

'I'll get right on it.'

'Seems strange that they would buy places in

Edinburgh and then buy a small hotel in the countryside in the middle of nowhere,' Max said.

'Maybe they just wanted to buy a place where their corporate clients could go away for a weekend without fear of a snooping photographer lying in wait,' Dan said.

'Let's look into the company further,' Craig said. 'I want to know who the top people are.' He looked at the photo of the dead woman that had been taken by Isla and printed out, then stuck on the board next to Goode's photo.

'Identifying the dead woman is going to be a bit trickier,' he said, turning back to the team.

'Dan explained that she was already dead and had been dug up out of her grave,' Max said.

Craig nodded. 'Aye. We need to find out why. Why dig up a woman out of her grave, put her in a room with a man and then kill the man? Set a wee fire, then put it out?'

'Maybe he was cold and just wanted some heat without it burning down the rest of the hotel,' Dan said, recalling the mini briefing he had given the other members of the team.

'Could be.' Craig looked at Max. 'Put some feelers out and see if there've been any similar cases in any of the other force areas.'

'I'll make some calls,' Max replied.

Craig looked over to their makeshift coffee station. 'Anybody snag some chocolate Hobnobs while they were out at the supermarket getting the new jar of coffee?'

'They're in the cupboard under the counter,' Gary said.

'They're not going to dish themselves out,' Isla said.

'You're closer to the cupboard than I am,' Gary said.

'Well, I'll just get up and get them then, shall I?' she said, standing up. 'Anybody else want one? Speak now or forever hold your peace.'

'I didn't bring a piece with me today,' Gary said, sniggering. 'I thought I'd just go to the canteen.'

'You're hilarious, Menzies.' Isla looked at the others. 'Going, going...'

'Aye, snag me a couple, Isla, thanks,' Max said. 'Ta.'

'No problem, sir. Dan? Jessie?'

'I shouldn't,' Dan said, a troubled look on his face. Have a couple of biscuits or worry about his carotid artery narrowing? The Hobnobs won out. 'Why not? Thanks.'

Jessie shook her head. 'No, thanks. I'm cutting back.'

Isla grabbed the biscuits and a small pile of paper napkins and brought the biscuits over. She was a stickler for having people eat the biscuits over an unfolded napkin so the crumbs were contained instead of getting jammed down the side of a key on a keyboard. The last time, it was *her* keyboard that somebody had sat at, eating and gobbing crumbs all over it. An unsuccessful half hour of chasing one crumb near the letter G had made her curse out the anonymous biscuit sprayer. The bastard.

Those who wanted a biscuit took one – or two – and a napkin, and they ate in silence for a few seconds, contemplating where the killer had got a cadaver from.

'There didn't appear to be any dirt on her, so he might have snagged her from a funeral director's,' Craig said. 'You know, sneaked in, unscrewed the lid, took her out and put the lid back so the coffin was empty when it was put into the ground.'

'Or burned,' Gary said, biting a biscuit in half. A cascade of crumbs fell onto the napkin. 'She might have been in line for cremation and they burned an empty coffin.'

Isla looked at him and just knew it was he who

had screwed up her keyboard. It hadn't been the same since that. The G made a slight clicking noise. Not a big deal, but then neither was a paper cut until you felt it every time you moved your hand.

Craig turned to Gary. 'If that were the case, then I'm sure they would have noticed the difference in weight. Unless he put something in to replace her. But my gut says that would take a lot of effort.'

'Easier to dig her up. Especially if the funeral was recent,' Isla said. 'The ground wouldn't have settled all the way.'

Craig turned to Max. 'Have it put in the system. Any desecrated grave discovered, I want to know about it.'

He finished his coffee and walked over to the coat stand and grabbed his jacket. 'I'm going to the mortuary to see how Annie is getting on. Then we'll go and talk to this Christopher Gregory guy. Isla, saddle up.'

FOUR

Glasgow

DCI Angie Fisher sat in her office in Helen Street station and looked at the salad in the plastic tub in front of her. 'Fucking rabbit food again.' It wouldn't have been so bad, but she'd made it herself before leaving the house that morning. She had told her husband-to-be that she was trying to slim down for their upcoming nuptials.

DI Dougie Fisher told her he liked her just the way she was, bless him. They had been married before, hence the same last name. He had lived in London for a while, but after they worked a case together in Scotland, she had known that despite hating him...she really didn't hate him at all. Was angry with him for cheating, but he had turned a corner. Besides, she had promised him that if he did it again, she'd cut his baws off.

Fisher had promised her that was all a thing of the past and that he was quite attached to his wedding tackle, both literally and figuratively. They had bandied about the idea of working at the same station, but after a sit-down with her boss, Det Sup Lynn McKenzie, Angie had thought maybe they should be posted at different stations. Angie was now at Helen Street, and Fisher was based in a CID office elsewhere in the city. He was content not being in MIT, and they were getting along better than they ever had, so why do anything that would fuck that up?

She prodded at the salad, poking at the lettuce and tomato until the fork speared a piece of each. Salad in November. Disgusting. Halloween had gone as she had expected it to: wee bastards coming round trick-or-treating, then still throwing eggs at the house. This was another Americanism that had reached across the Atlantic. What next? Saying 'You're welcome' when somebody thanked you? She couldn't see that going down well in the Gorbals. Or anywhere else in Scotland.

Her phone rang. A welcome distraction from eating the salad.

'DCI Fisher,' she said, picking up the handset.

'Good afternoon, ma'am, this is DI Max Hold, Fife Division.'

Angie looked at her wall clock. Half past midday. The morning had charged away from her like a steam train.

'Afternoon, DI Hold. How can I help you?'

'We're working a case up here, and I did a quick search on the internet and found a story near you that's similar to ours.'

Angie sat forward. 'Interesting. Tell me more.'

Max explained about the bodies being found in the hotel.

'When did we have a similar case here? I wasn't always at Helen Street.'

'It was about two years ago. Two bodies were found in a house fire. The house had been completely gutted, but one of the victims was found to have died from stab wounds. The other one looked like...well, this is going to sound strange, but it's like our case: the female looked like she was already dead when the fire was set. I called the mortuary at the Queen Elizabeth to confirm.' He filled her in on some details.

'I haven't heard about that, but as I said, I haven't been here that long. Let me look into it and I'll get back to you.'

'Thank you, ma'am.'

Angie hung up and sat back in her chair. Two bodies found in a burnt-out house? She sprang forward again and started a search on her computer. Up it came, the case notes about the fire.

She stood up, grabbing her jacket from behind her chair, and walked into the incident room. She spotted the sergeant she was looking for, sitting at his computer.

DS Robbie Evans.

'Robbie? I can see you're busy, but I'd like you to come with me.'

Evans stood up. 'Yes, ma'am. Can I ask where we're going?'

'You can ask. I'll even let you drive. In fact, Hamish?'

The young, ginger-headed detective looked at her like she was about to give out doughnuts. 'Ma'am?'

'You can come along for the ride.'

DC Connor grabbed hold of his jacket from the back of his chair as he stood up. He looked at Evans, who just shrugged, and then they left the station. Angie tossed Evans the car keys.

'We're going to a burnt-out wreck in Paisley. I'll put the address into the satnav.' She briefly explained what they were doing.

They got into her car, with Evans driving, Angie in the passenger seat and Hamish in the back, where he could stay out of mischief.

Evans took off, listening to the directions, heading out onto the M8. The sky was the colour of something a dog might throw up if he'd eaten plasterboard.

'Did you have any of those kids who dress up knocking on your door last night?' Angie asked both men, still smarting at the one wee bastard who'd been dressed as Spider-Man.

'Aye, my mum nearly shat herself when one of them pointed a knife at her,' Evans said. 'Turned out it was a fake rubber one. She told him she'd ram it up his arse.'

'Good for her. How about you, Hame?'

Hamish looked forward. He'd been thinking about his Harry Potter Lego set again. There was a piece missing, he was sure of it, and no matter how good a detective he was, he couldn't track the thing down. He'd narrowed down his list of suspects: the dog, one of his nephews or actually himself. He'd been scranning a tube of Pringles and had stuffed more into his mouth than he could handle and had coughed them all over the dining table, where his latest creation sat. In his haste to sweep up the mixture of wet and not-quite-so-wet bits of chewed crisps (Were they crisps? Crisps or flattened potatoes that some robot had sat on to give them their curly shape) maybe he had inadvertently caught a piece of the shaped plastic in his waiting hand at the edge of the table. He had several options: wait to see if the dog crapped out the piece; threaten his nephew, the bad wee bastard one; rake about in the bin after he'd emptied the vacuum cleaner into it; or write to Lego explaining what a twat he'd been. An adult twat, no less. Maybe he could invent another adult who lived in the house, somebody like a fictitious wife, and he could write to Lego and blame it on her.

Dear Lego, my wife's a twat.

'Hamish?' Angie said, snapping him to the here and now. 'Ground Control to Hamish. Come in, Hamish.'

'Sorry, boss, I was miles away there. I was trying to think if I'd heard about those bodies.'

Angie turned to look at him. 'Liar. You're pulling a beamer. You know your face turns the same colour as your heid when you lie.' She tutted. 'Were you thinking about your bloody Lego again?'

'I've lost a piece of my Harry Potter train,' he complained. 'I think my dug ate it. Or my girlfriend.'

'Your dug ate your girlfriend?' Evans said, grinning, looking at his colleague in the rearview mirror.

'That's it, laugh it up. But it will cock the whole thing up. I'll need to write to Lego and ask them for another piece, and who knows when they'll send it out. And I'm already getting grief from Frances about taking up the dining room table with what she calls "toys".' Hamish shook his head. 'That's sacrilege. Bloody toys.'

'Anyway, I was asking if you'd had any of those trick-or-treaters last night?' Angie said. 'And don't have me asking you again.'

'I did. I gave them some sweets just to get rid of them. One bloke turned up wearing a boiler suit and wearing a Michael Myers mask. He said he was with the wee laddies and that one of them was his grandson, but he took a handful of sweeties. And his hands were huge. Could probably have scooped out the whole bowl if I'd let him.'

'You didn't question him?' Angie said, her eyebrows knitting together.

'Well...you know...I had to get back to my Lego.'

Angie turned back to look out of the windscreen, all thoughts of psychos and toys for older boys slipping out of her head, as Evans was getting closer. 'I need a holiday. A week in Tenerife sounds about right. I wish Doogie was taking me.'

'I'm sure he'll take you somewhere nice for your honeymoon,' Hamish offered from the back seat.

'You never know. Maybe a wee trip to New York, right after the wedding. Summer over there would be good. Not like this pish,' Angie said, looking out at the big houses that had appeared on her left. She looked forward. 'I think it's up here on the right. You go in a wee driveway that's shared with the housing complex,' she said, pointing to it as the satnav told them they had arrived.

Evans indicated and turned right into what was really a small road off Stevenson Road.

'Up ahead,' Hamish said, leaning forward and pointing.

'Aye, I think we can see where it is, Hamish,' Angie said. 'What gave it away? The big black hole where the roof used to be?'

'Sometimes those satnav things get it wrong, boss,' Hamish complained. 'That's what my girlfriend says when she's driving and we get lost.'

'I bet she also says you're a fantastic lover, that

some men can actually manage it after they've been drinking and that five minutes is *not* a world record,' Angie said, opening the passenger door when Evans had stopped the car.

'Six minutes, but who's counting?' Hamish mumbled as he too opened his door.

'It doesn't count when the clock's ticking and you're trying to get your boots off,' Angie said, closing her door.

'Feel free to jump in anytime and back me up on this, Robbie,' Hamish complained as he shut his door and Evans climbed out from behind the wheel.

'Don't bring me into your filth.' Evans made a face at his colleague.

'Now, now, boys, let's have a bit of concentration here,' Angie said, standing with her hands on her hips, looking at the large building in front of her. It had obviously grown from its original footprint over the years, having been turned into a nursing home before its demise. It was red stone at the front, with a modern addition on one side that extended round the back. Angie had checked the image on Google Earth before leaving the office. The addition had been built by Eyesore & Sons, Contractors.

She walked closer to the old building, staring up at the roof. One half was balanced precariously on the stone edge, while the other half was mostly gone, a few blackened timbers pointing skywards.

'What happened here?' Evans asked as the three of them now looked at the building.

'Two bodies were found after the fire was put out. The male subject had been stabbed before the fire was set. The female was already dead when the fire was lit.'

Evans and Hamish both looked at her.

'Dead?' Evans said. 'Like she had been murdered too?'

Angie shivered for a moment, as if the ghosts of the two victims had come out to walk over her. Then she looked at Evans. 'No. Like she was already dead when he took her in there. There was no soot in her lungs.'

'Already dead?' Hamish said, a confused look on his face. 'Like she'd been murdered somewhere else?'

Angie turned to him. 'No. Like she was already dead. Just dead. DI Max Hold from Fife called the Queen Elizabeth Hospital and spoke to somebody in pathology. They told him the girl had had a ruptured spleen and died on the operating table.'

'Jesus,' Evans said. 'I wonder how he managed to get her out of the hospital and up here?'

'Maybe she wasn't taken from the hospital,'

Angie said. 'Maybe from the funeral parlour, or...' She shook her head, not quite believing the words that were going to come out of her mouth next. The wind slightly ruffled her short hair as she stood looking at the beast of a house. 'Or he dug her up.'

She walked forward, the two other detectives following her. The building had been boarded up on the ground floor, with a notice warning people that it was dangerous and not to enter. She started walking round the left-hand side of the building, on a driveway that had seen better days. The wind rattled the trees and the sky was the colour of an old boiler.

She turned round, but the other two detectives weren't behind her. It was almost as if they had vanished off the face of the earth. But then they turned the corner. She admitted to herself that she was relieved to see them. Angie turned the corner and reached the extension that had been tacked on many years ago.

'The kitchens and delivery entrance,' she said, pointing to a sign. 'Laundry too. Big doors to get delivery trolleys and carts through. He could have brought her through here.'

'What about the man?' Hamish said. 'Do you think the killer brought them both through here?'

'He did. But the man was alive when he was

brought in here. There was smoke in his lungs, so they know he was breathing before he died in there.'

'It has to still be an open case,' Evans said.

'It is. I checked. But after two years, it ran cold.' She turned to Evans. 'When we get back, I'd like you both to put aside what you're working on for today and see if you can find a connection between our two victims and one of the two victims they have in Fife.'

'I'm assuming they haven't identified the other one?' Evans said.

'Correct,' Angie said. 'The one they did identify used to be one of us a long time ago. Fife Constabulary. But he wasn't cut out for the job and turned to nursing instead.'

'Still dealing with death,' Evans said, 'just in a different way.'

'Aye, well, his partner was stabbed and he legged it. He was better off quitting the job before he got somebody killed.'

They had one last look at the old building before walking back round to the car.

FIVE

'I still don't know if you're hungover or if you're just feeling your age,' Isla said, smiling at Craig from the driving seat of the Volvo as she swung the car into the Tim Hortons at Fife Leisure Park.

'We should buy shares in this place,' he said, ignoring her comment.

Rain spat on the windscreen, and the sky was dark and foreboding. Craig wondered if one day he would open the curtains to find a mist outside and everything else gone. Or maybe see the neighbours eating each other. Something from the mind of Stephen King come true.

'To be honest, boss, you probably wouldn't have made it all the way to Inverness without letting Annie drive. And we all know how she drives.' They got out and Isla locked the car. 'Probably would have got there in half the time, mind.'

'I could always have taken some sleeping tablets.'

'How would you have had fun on your dirty weekend away if you did that?'

'Can you keep your mind out of the gutter for one bloody minute?' Craig said as they went from the cold into the warmth of the coffee shop.

'You having a doughnut?' she asked him. 'My treat.'

'As much as I'd like to, I'd rather not be lying on Annie's table in the near future.'

'Aye, me neither. Got to stay trim.'

'For who?' Craig said. 'A boyfriend?'

'Nobody special. Well, we've been chatting online. He's great. We're both gamers and he's into crime.'

Craig raised his eyebrows. 'Gamer? I didn't know that about you, Isla. I thought you were happy playing with your cat?'

'Funny. It's a way of destressing. I play live games, the kind where I carry a big sword and wipe out invading armies. Just like chucking-out time on a Saturday night. Anyway, we got chatting and he's a nice guy.'

Craig looked at her for a second. 'I hate to piss on your parade, but he could be catfishing.'

She gave a short laugh, more of a snort. 'I know that. But we've FaceTimed. He's real. He hasn't asked me for money.'

'What does he do for a living?'

'He works in the media. Sort of. He does a podcast called *Bark and Hair*. It's a true-crime podcast and he has his dog with him. It's a play on words. Burke and Hare, the famous Edinburgh killers who dug up bodies –'

Craig held up a hand, interrupting her. 'I'm up to speed on who Burke and Hare were.'

They ordered the coffees – an extra one for Annie, who would say, 'Aw, I wish I'd known you were going there,' making them feel guilty – and Craig asked for extra milk.

'Maybe he was just trying to impress you, and he still lives with his mother,' Craig said, taking his cup of coffee from the server, hoping she'd remembered the extra milk. He didn't want a repeat of Gary Menzies' coffee, which tasted like he'd heated it up in a blast furnace.

'I don't think so, sir,' Isla said, sipping her coffee and holding Annie's in her other hand. 'I didn't get that impression.'

'What's this guy's name?' Craig asked.

Isla smiled. 'Ian Bark. Hence the name in the title. You should take a listen. I think you would enjoy it. You might even like him if I decide to introduce you to him when he gets here.'

'You never know,' Craig said. He had every intention of listening to the man's show.

He held the door open for her and they left, Craig wondering if he should mention to her boyfriend that she had a nice smile when she was happy, told a good dirty joke, had a good sense of humour and would go the extra mile when a colleague needed help. And that he, Craig, knew some people who would be very upset if Isla got pissed about.

'I can tell this guy makes you happy,' Craig said, not quite willing to let it go yet.

'He does,' she said, handing him Annie's coffee while she fished out the car keys. 'It's nothing serious just now. We're just having fun, then we'll see where it goes from here.'

'You said, "when he gets here". Where's he coming from? Edinburgh?'

'A little further. It's sort of a long-distance relationship. He lives in London.'

'London? It could be worse,' Craig said.

She nodded. 'I knew somebody who started a relationship with somebody in America. At least I could get on a train. But he's making the first move. He's coming up for a visit.'

She blipped the fob, and he waited until she'd got behind the wheel before handing her Annie's coffee. She put the two cups in the cup holders as he walked round to the other side.

'Maybe me and the boys could take him for a couple of pints,' Craig said, settling into the car and managing to look like a halfwit as he put the seat belt on without spilling his coffee over himself. 'Det Sup Calvin Stewart knows a few good places.'

'Who?' she said, and she drove out of the car park like Annie had been giving her lessons.

'Never mind. Maybe it's best you don't meet him.'

SIX

Annie was in the autopsy suite when Craig rolled in with Isla trailing behind. Annie was standing at one of the stainless-steel tables, the naked body of the female victim from the hotel lying on it. The other table held the male victim, a sheet pulled up to his head.

Isla had stopped briefly to talk to a uniformed officer she knew, a young man who was there interviewing somebody regarding a car crash.

'A friend of yours?' Craig said.

'We were in uniform together. He knows Jessie. He'll be at the do tonight. I think he has a thing for her, but he's a bit shy and hasn't plucked up the courage to ask her out.'

'And now she's leaving,' Annie said.

'Back to Glasgow, where she originates from. Her old dad is poorly and she wants to spend as much time with him as possible. So she's going back there.'

'Good for her,' Craig said. 'Maybe Isla will find somebody tonight, if her other guy doesn't work out.'

Annie looked at him. 'Is this you trying to pair that poor girl off with one of those old fuckwits? She needs a young man her own age, not some old duffer who has more golf clubs than grandkids.' Annie looked at Isla. 'Don't listen to him, sweetheart. Just because he's going out with one of the best-looking medical professionals this side of the Forth Bridge.'

Craig nodded, feeling like they were ganging up on him now and he was taking part in a reality show where the first wrong answer could lead to you having your nuts cut off. 'Forth Bridge,' he said.

Annie smiled. 'See? I told you.'

'I'm not in a hurry,' Isla said. 'Besides, Ian is just a friend. Who knows where it will lead after he comes up.'

'Good for you. Just remember, Auntie Annie is here to look after you.'

'Thank you, Annie. At least you didn't call me a crack whore.'

'A fucking what?' Annie looked at Craig. 'No, you didn't.'

'I didn't say that!' He drank more coffee.

'Not in so many words.' Isla looked at Annie. 'He said I have a cat.'

Annie looked at Craig. 'You bastard.'

Craig shook his head. It was like being caught in the middle of a comedy act rehearsing their routine. 'Don't listen to her.'

Isla laughed. 'I told him about my friend who I met online.'

'You did?' Annie said.

'You knew about this and didn't tell me?' Craig said.

'Of course. When we said, no secrets, this doesn't count. This is girls' talk.'

'Anyway, you said you had something to show us,' Craig said, changing the subject as he felt he was about to turn a dark corner.

'I do indeed. Have a look at this.' Annie pointed with a gloved finger at the woman's ankle. They all saw a tattoo there. Three words: *I love Jesus*.

'I've left the others trawling through obituary sites online,' Craig said, 'to see if they can come up with an obit that has her photo in it.'

'Have you opened her up again?' Isla asked.

'Oh, yes. It was one of my easier ones. Her organs had been put back inside her after the first postmortem. It looks like she had a heart attack. Probably a sudden death since she looks to be in her thirties.'

'I know it can happen to anybody, but it's always sad when it happens to a younger person,' Isla said.

'Any idea of how long she's been dead?' Craig asked Annie.

'She's been embalmed, and quite well, actually, so it's hard to narrow it down. But her hands are a bit dried out, so a little while. I would say, and don't quote me on this, around a year to eighteen months.'

'Maybe we could put that in our search parameters,' Craig said, turning round to Isla, but she was gone. 'Where did she go?'

Annie put a hand on his arm. 'You've still got a lot to learn about women, my dear. Maybe she's away to talk to that uniform.'

'I think some guys have been pulling her chain at the golf club,' Craig said. 'Isla, I mean.'

'Not in front of me. Not if they know what's good for them.' Annie smiled, but there was something in her eyes that told him it wouldn't be a pleasant experience for the recipient if she let fly.

'I'll talk to her in the car.' He tossed his empty

coffee cup in a waste basket. 'I was just wise-cracking when I said she had a cat.'

'Jimmy. What were you thinking, calling her a cat lady at her age?'

'I wasn't. That's the problem. But anyway, have you had a chance to think about Richard Goode over there?' He nodded to the other corpse.

'I asked around and it seems somebody here worked with him a while back; they were in Dundee together. He remembers bumping into Goode back in the summer. Goode said he was working in a private nursing home now. Better money, better conditions.'

'I don't suppose he said where?'

'No. He's not even sure that Goode mentioned it.'

'Never mind,' Craig said, 'we'll look him up. I have Jessie looking for a next of kin.'

'If he was as bad as Mark Baker said, then there should be no shortage of uniforms who remember him.'

'It was twenty-five years ago. A lot of them will have moved on by now. But we're asking anyway.' He looked at his watch. 'I have to go now. I want to track down somebody who was at our crime scene three years ago.'

'Okay. I'll keep you posted.'

Craig was about to leave the mortuary, but then he stopped. 'Did you know Isla was a gamer?'

Annie looked puzzled. 'A gamer? You mean, she sits and plays video games?'

'Aye, like that.'

Annie shook her head. 'That's news to me.'

Craig nodded. 'Maybe she's a closet gamer or something.'

'Maybe. I'll ask her.'

Craig reached out and put a hand on her arm. 'Don't. She told me in confidence.'

'Okay, sweetheart.'

'See you after work?' Craig asked. 'My place. Before we go out to celebrate Jessie moving on.'

'Christ, don't make it sound like she died,' Annie said.

Craig waved a hand as he left.

SEVEN

London

DS Leanne Chalmers sat back in her office chair and pulled open the desk drawer for what seemed like the millionth time. She looked around the office at the others, but nobody was paying her any attention.

She slipped the postcard out again. She hadn't bothered taking this one to the lab. The last five had no prints on them and she supposed this one wouldn't either.

She turned it over in her hands and read the handwritten message again:

. . .

Hello again, Leanne.

So sorry to hear you're leaving. Scotland's going to be a bit chilly this time of year, isn't it? Still, you'll get used to it. I'll be sorry to see you go. It's been great playing the game with you. Remember Spain? We had so much fun! Not sure I want to let this go, though. I'll give it some thought.

Best to Sonia when you see her.

The Traveller

A little hand-drawn suitcase had been added. Just like on the rest of them.

'Remember Spain?' Had he followed her out there when she had gone on holiday with her friends? If he had, he had watched from afar. She didn't believe it, but then, how did he know she'd gone there?

She put the postcard back in the drawer, along with the other five. Her gaffer, Detective Superintendent Louis Todd, hadn't taken them seriously. He had told her that it was somebody pulling her chain. The Traveller was a man they had hunted, chased, and they had watched as he fell off a bridge into the river below to be swept away.

'He was never found,' Leanne had reminded him.

Todd was of the old school. 'Bring me proof,' he had told her, dismissing it out of hand.

She had lain awake in her new flat for many a night, running things through her mind. Had she missed something? A man bumping into her at the train station, perhaps? Somebody standing next to her as she ordered her overpriced coffee? Walking around the grocery store? He could have been watching her anywhere.

Her thoughts turned to her mother, Sonia. Victim number seven of the killer known as The Traveller. Not some gawdy name created by the media, but one he signed himself.

He would leave a postcard by his victim, as if he had sent it to a friend, and he'd sign it 'The Traveller'. No card ever had the same handwriting, but each one had a little drawing of a suitcase, also drawn slightly differently each time so as not to give a signature.

Det Sup Todd had told her that the person who was sending her these cards was probably somebody she had pissed off and who knew about the case. It was all over the media, so it shouldn't come as a surprise, he said, that some fruitcake was targeting her.

Leanne wasn't convinced. Her mother had been the last victim, murdered eight months earlier. Before The Traveller had supposedly died four weeks later. The first postcard had been sent to Leanne a month later, then one each month. She wondered why she was being targeted. Why postcards? Had the other victims been sent cards before their deaths? None had ever been found.

'You look like you could do with a drink, girl,' DCI Mike Lewis said, putting a hand on her shoulder. He was touching fifty, tall and lean, with hair that was holding on to its colour for as long as possible while the sideburns slowly gave in to the advancing grey.

She smiled at him. 'I won't argue with that.'

'Go on then, get that bottle out that you keep hidden away in your drawer. Have a good chug of it. Nobody will say anything, especially since this is your last day.'

She laughed. 'First of all, I wish there was a bottle in there, and secondly, I'm hitting the road early tomorrow morning.'

'I thought you were taking the train up there?'

'Figure of speech, boss. I sold my car and now I'll

be on the lookout for another one, but I don't want to be sitting on the train with a splitting headache, looking for somewhere to puke.'

'That's the spirit. But we're still taking you to the pub. DI Cargill is going to put his hand in his pocket for once.'

Sean Cargill looked over at the boss and shook his head. 'You're the one making the big bucks, boss; maybe you could break that ten-shilling note you keep in your wallet.'

'Listen to that cheeky little bastard. I'll make sure you're spending your dosh tonight, my old son. This lady is heading north tomorrow and we want to give her a good send-off.' Lewis looked down at Leanne, still sitting in her chair. 'Don't you worry, you won't have to put your hand in your pocket.'

She smiled. 'Thanks, boss.'

He lowered his voice. 'You taking those postcards with you?'

Her smile dropped a bit. 'I might as well. They've been to forensics, and Det Sup Todd doesn't seem to think they're related to the real Traveller. He thinks it's somebody trying to rattle me.'

'He may well be right, Leanne. Besides, our man took a dive into a river and never came back up. Heavy rain for days, swollen river, fast running.'

'He should have come up somewhere, boss.'

'There were no more victims. We searched his house and found a stack of blank postcards all showing the same thing: touristy London. And there were trophies in his attic, things his mother swore weren't there before.'

'I know, boss. I wish I hadn't been taken off the case,' Leanne said, her mind going back to finding her mother strangled on her bed, the necktie pulled tight. One of the neckties used in the murders had had a name on it, and they had traced the guy, but he had sworn he had given it to a charity shop. He also had an iron-clad alibi. That was when they knew The Traveller was shopping for ties in charity shops. And if he was getting ties, then he was probably getting clothes there to wear to the murder scenes.

They got their lucky break when forensics pulled a thumbprint from the last scene. It belonged to convicted paedophile Thomas Whittaker. They had gone to his house en masse, with Mike Lewis leading the charge. He had promised to keep Leanne in the loop and FaceTime her as they brought the bastard out, but when they smashed the door off its hinges, they found Whittaker was gone.

His mother said her son had received a phone call a few minutes beforehand and had scarpered.

Lewis had then spotted Whittaker heading for a local park, and they had descended on it and given chase. Whittaker had a head start, but Lewis ran every morning and competed in marathons, and he soon caught up.

'Thomas!' Lewis had shouted.

Torchlight cut through the darkness and pissing rain, landing on Whittaker. He was standing on the edge of the footbridge crossing the river. It had been raining hard for days and the water below was high and fast-moving.

'Fuck off!' he shouted. 'I'm not going back to prison! I never touched those women!'

'Come on down, son! We'll help you,' Lewis said.

Whittaker locked eyes with him through the dark. Lewis told the uniform not to blind the bastard as Whittaker put a hand up to shield his face.

Then he fell backward into the rushing water. And was never seen again.

'He knew why we were there, Leanne,' Lewis said now, looking down at her once more. 'He knew we were there to arrest him for the murders. His print was at the scene.'

'Bit convenient, sir, if you don't mind me saying.'

'I don't mind at all,' Lewis said, smiling. 'It's Todd who'll have a fucking coronary. But we've always wondered who called Whittaker. The call came from a call box in Ealing. No cameras anywhere nearby.'

Leanne looked at him. 'Do you still think it's an inside job?'

Lewis shrugged. 'It's the only thing that makes sense. Unless one of us spoke out of turn to the wrong person. That can happen. But it has to be somebody close to the case.'

'Somebody who knows I'm moving to Scotland.'

'What about that ex-boyfriend of yours?'

'Not Ian. Besides, I met him after I started receiving the postcards. And I ran him through the system, even though we're not supposed to.'

Lewis grinned. 'We all do it. Force of habit.'

'He came up clean. And he was a great guy. It was me who dumped him, and last I heard, he'd moved on. He does podcasts with his new girlfriend. I can't see why he'd be sending me the postcards.'

'You know I'll always have your back, Leanne,' Lewis said.

'I know that, boss. Even from south of the border.'

'Right then, let's get our work done for the day and make sure our little incident room is all spick and span before we head off to the pub later,' Lewis said, raising his voice.

There was mumbling around the room as Lewis went into his office.

Leanne gave her desk drawer one more look before getting back to work.

EIGHT

There was a motorcycle half covered by a ratty plastic tarp in the front garden of Christopher Gregory's house. The gate squeaked as Craig opened it, and he walked up the path to the front door. The path itself was made of flagstones, some of which had moved, creating a trip hazard.

Craig knocked loudly on the uPVC door.

'Nice place,' Isla said. Craig turned to see her making a face. 'This would get on the cover of *Homes and Gardens* for sure.'

'I've been to worse places, let me tell you,' Craig said, turning back to the door and rapping the brass door knocker this time.

'Fuckin' comin'. Give me soddin' minute!' came a shout from inside.

'And there, ladies and gentlemen, is the reason young Christopher spent time in the big house,' Craig said, turning to Isla again.

The door was flung open and an older man stood looking at them. 'What the fuck do you want?'

Craig looked at him. 'DCI James Craig. DS McGregor. We'd like a word with Christopher Gregory. Is he in?'

'What's the wee bastard done now?'

'Are you related to him?' Craig asked.

'I'm his fuckin' father, pal. Unfortunately, I am indeed related to him.'

'What's your name, sir?' Craig asked.

'Les Gregory. His mother should have let me give the bastard a good belting when he was younger. Maybe he would have stayed out of trouble then.'

'Is he in?' Craig asked again.

'Aye. He's in his fuckin' pit.' The man walked away, indicating for them to come into the house 'before all the fuckin' heat gets out', so Craig and Isla walked in, Isla closing the door.

It was a terraced house belonging to the Fife council, and while a lot of people kept their house neat and tidy, the same couldn't be said for Gregory Senior. The place smelled like an ashtray mixed with a wee dollop of last week's Chinese takeout.

'Chris!' Les shouted. 'Get out your fuckin' bed! The pi...polis are here to see you!' He turned to Craig and Isla. 'Lazy wee bastard.'

They heard a thump from upstairs, a pair of feet hitting the floor, then a door opening.

'What's the racket down there?'

'Polis are here to see you.'

'Aww fuck. What now?'

'How do I fuckin' know? They want to speak to you, not me. Get your arse down here.'

They heard Junior tutting and then his feet thumping on the stairs. When he reached the bottom step, he stopped and looked at both detectives.

'What you been doing now, ye wee bastard?' Les said.

'Nothin'. Not a bloody thing.'

'DCI Craig, DS McGregor,' Craig said.

Christopher mumbled something unintelligible before stepping down onto the hallway floor. He was dressed in a t-shirt and boxer shorts, and his hair looked like it was a wig made out of a badger. He yawned and scratched his balls.

Isla looked at Craig and made a face. She wouldn't be shaking the young man's hand on the way out, and assumed it was likewise for Craig.

'Get through to the living room,' Les said. 'Then

you can get your arse down the job centre instead of lying in your hole all morning.'

'You should try that,' Christopher said.

'Hey, this is my fuckin' house. Besides, I'm disabled.'

'Phhh,' Christopher said, and Les's eyes went wide for a moment, like he was thinking some other nonsense was going to come out of his son's mouth.

'Living room. Now.'

Christopher went through a doorway, and the detectives followed after Les indicated for them to do so.

It wasn't the cowp that Craig was expecting. The faux-leather settee looked new, or maybe new-ish, if it had come via somebody else's living room. The TV was big, but what house didn't have a big TV nowadays? Two chairs were positioned at an angle to the TV, mismatched and not leather, faux or otherwise. A china cabinet sat against a side wall, glass doors revealing Wally Dugs and other pieces of what the *Antiques Roadshow* would have pissed themselves at.

'Have a pew,' Les said, following them in. They sat on the couch, which creaked and grumbled at their combined weight.

Christopher lounged in a chair, his legs dangling

over the side. 'What's up, then?' he said, looking at Craig.

'Is Mrs Gregory around?' Isla asked.

'Neither of you two worked the case three years ago, did you?' Les asked, rhetorically.

Craig looked at the man. He was on the short side, around five seven, Craig guessed, but what he didn't have in stature, he made up for in mouth. His hair was shaved down to the skin, and his face had been on the receiving end of a few knuckles in its time.

Craig gave the man a look that suggested he might take even more interest in Les Gregory if he didn't stop speaking in tongues.

Les shrugged. 'She buggered off with the postie years ago. It's just me and him now.'

'And that slag,' Christopher said.

'You watch your fuckin' mouth,' Les said, pointing a finger at his son. Then he turned his attention to Craig. 'My girlfriend doesn't see eye to eye with my offspring.'

'That's putting it mildly,' Christopher said under his breath, but loud enough for them all to hear.

'We want to ask you about the Gateway Hotel,' Craig said.

'Not this shite again,' Christopher said, sitting

up and swinging his feet round to plant them on the floor in front of the chair. 'I told you lot back then I wouldn't grass up my mates, and I still won't.'

'Being stuck in your bed, you might not have heard,' Craig said.

'What's that then? Somebody went back to finish the job?' Christopher grinned at his father.

'Yes,' Isla said simply.

Christopher's smile dropped off his face like it had been too heavy and he couldn't keep hold of it anymore. 'What do you mean?'

'Two people were found dead in the hotel this morning. And the circumstances lead us to believe that you might have been there, Christopher,' Craig said, his eyes locking on to the young man's.

'Wait a minute, I wasn't at the hotel. I've been in prison.'

'You weren't in prison when this happened,' Craig said, careful not to reveal when the fire had been started.

'I've never been back to that hotel since the night I fell and broke my leg. I admitted to starting the fire, but it wasn't malicious. We were just cold, and smoking and drinking. The bastards put me away, though. I did my time.'

'He did his time,' Les said, as if the detectives hadn't heard at first.

Craig looked at him. 'Why don't you sit down, Mr Gregory?'

Les was about to argue, but then saw it was pointless and sat on the other chair.

'Where were you last night?' Isla asked Christopher.

'Whoa, whoa, does he need a lawyer here now? You're questioning him and you haven't read him his rights,' Les said.

Craig thought that the father might have been a good candidate for the *Jeremy Kyle Show*, had it still been running.

'Right now, Christopher is just helping us with our enquiries, seeing as how he has intimate knowledge of the building,' Craig said. 'But if you want a lawyer present, we can arrange for him to meet us at the station, where I can formally charge your son with murder.' It was a bluff. Craig didn't have enough evidence to charge the boy, but neither the father nor the son knew this.

'Aw, waiting a fuckin' minute,' Les said, and for a moment, Craig thought the man had seen through his bluff.

'Or you can tell us where you were last night,

Christopher, and give us the names of the friends you were with that night three years ago.'

Christopher looked like the wind had been taken out of his sails, and he looked down at the floor. 'I can't.' He looked back up, making eye contact with Craig. 'Give you their names, I mean. Last night, I was here, with him. We watched TV, had a few tinnies, then I went to my room and did some online gaming.'

'Really?' Isla said, managing to keep the scepticism in her voice, but inwardly, she was intrigued. 'What game?'

'*Battle of Orr*,' Christopher said. 'I know, it's geeky, but since I got out of prison, nobody will give me a job. They all think I'll burn their place down.'

'What's your moniker?' Isla asked.

Christopher looked at her with suspicion for a moment before sensing that she wasn't asking to try to trap him.

'Vulcan24,' Christopher answered. 'Roman god of fire.'

Isla quickly looked at Craig before looking at Christopher. 'I think I'm your alibi,' she said.

They stared at her.

'What do you mean?' Christopher asked finally.

'I play *Battle of Orr* too.'

'You?' Christopher said.

'Athena3420.' Isla looked at Craig. 'It's Mr Boots' birthday. Third of April,' she elaborated, in case her boss couldn't work it out for himself.

'You know him?' Craig asked.

Isla nodded. 'I play that game all the time, and Mr Gregory and I have been competing for the last month or so. Every night, almost, including last night.'

'It might have been the old boy playing for all we know,' Craig said.

'Hey, less of the old,' Les warned, making a face.

'Him?' Christopher said. 'Play an online game? He can barely use the remote for the TV.' He smiled and laughed.

Isla laughed.

'I'm right here,' Les complained.

'This is brilliant,' Christopher said, sitting forward showing Isla a newfound respect. 'You know what time I was playing until.'

Isla looked at her boss. 'Almost two o'clock this morning.'

Craig looked at the young man. 'In your bedroom?'

'Aye. Go up and have a look. The Xbox is in there at a wee desk. I don't have any friends anymore. Not since...well, you know.' The smile dropped for a moment. 'It's why I spend most of my time at home.'

Craig nodded to Isla, who got up off the couch. 'Which room is yours?' she asked Christopher.

'Second door on the landing. Next to Snorey McFarter.' He beamed at her. 'That should be *his* moniker.'

Isla smiled as she left the room.

Craig looked at Christopher. 'Why can't you give me their names? The friends you were with the night of the fire.'

Christopher looked at him. 'They're dead. Giving you their names won't make any difference.'

'Dead? How?'

Christopher clocked his father and then looked back at Craig. 'They died in a house fire. In an old, abandoned place. That's what I heard. It happened when I was inside. They were probably in there smoking weed or something, and the place went up and they died. The police said it was an accident.'

'When exactly did this happen?' Craig asked.

'Eighteen months ago.'

'Whereabouts?' Craig sat forward in his chair.

'In some abandoned farmhouse somewhere. I'm not exactly sure where.'

Craig took a deep breath and sighed. 'Their names are going to be part of the record now. Why don't you just tell me?'

'It just feels like I would be betraying them.'

'You wouldn't be. You would be helping me,' Craig said.

Christopher looked at his father again and Les nodded.

'Peter Swanson and Robert Goode.'

'Goode?' Craig said. 'Any relation to Richard Goode?'

Christopher nodded. 'Aye. That was his dad.'

NINE

Craig was tired. He told Isla this and she was quite happy to drive the Volvo. Craig thought he might let her drive more often. Catch a power nap.

'Athena3420,' he said, looking sideways at her as she powered the car along the M90. 'I never took you as a gamer.'

'We all have our little secrets, boss,' Isla said. 'Besides, I could be doing worse things with my time: drinking, gambling, drugs.'

'You say that like they're bad things,' Craig said, looking forward again.

'Is that why London's so bad?' she said, risking a quick look at him before eyes forward. 'Drugs?'

'I was jesting of course. And you're right, there

are worse ways to pass your time. And Mr Boots must be so proud.'

'My cat lies on my desk when I'm playing, I'll have you know.'

'I'm not knocking it.' He chewed on a corner of his thumbnail, wondering where he would spit the little kernel if he bit it off, then thought better of it. 'And it was definitely Christopher Gregory you were playing against last night?'

Isla nodded. 'It was his gamer tag. I mean, if we stripped this down, we could go off on a tangent. His father really could be halfway intelligent and just acting like a doughnut. Or Christopher really could have a friend and he had that friend come round and play as him while Christopher was out murdering his friend's father. But where would he have got a dead body? We're going round in circles on this one, boss. Funeral parlour? Grave? Take your pick.'

Craig was staring out of the windscreen at the traffic heading north, deep in thought. He looked at Isla for a moment. 'Take the A91, Isla. Go past the hotel we were at this morning.'

Isla looked puzzled but did as she was asked. Ten minutes later, they slowed down for the A912. A patrol car was blocking the road. Craig showed his ID and was waved through. The forensics team were still at the scene, but Craig knew it wouldn't be long before they were packing their equipment away for the day.

There was no other traffic on the road except for another patrol car down at the hotel. Once again, Craig showed his ID, and he saw the emergency vehicles were blocking the road and the diversion wouldn't be lifted until it was clear.

'Turn right, Isla. According to Google, it's a twelve-minute drive. Seven miles. If Goode was brought from his home under duress, this would be the way his killer would have come. At least, it's the way I would have come.'

She nodded and turned right, keeping the Volvo at a reasonable speed on the twisty roads. They turned from the A912 onto the A913, passing through Abernethy and heading on to Newburgh. Finally, Isla turned off the main road into Abbey Road. Craig imagined John, Paul, Ringo and George walking across in front of them, then the image vanished.

The house they were looking for was on the left. A field was opposite, with a small distillery further up. The street was worlds away from its counterpart in London. Hills were shrouded by low clouds in the distance, and rain started coming down as Craig and

Isla got out of the car and walked up the path to the semi-detached house. There was a car in the small driveway at the side, blocking the path of a caravan.

Craig had tasked Max Hold with delivering the death message, and a family liaison officer had been appointed. It was the FLO who answered the door, before they got there.

'PC Edwards, DCI Craig,' she said.

'How do you know who I am?' Craig asked.

'DI Hold said you would be coming, along with DS McGregor. Besides, I've seen you in the station.' She looked back into the house for a second. 'The neighbour and the minister are here as well.'

'Ah. Right then, let us in,' Craig said.

Edwards ushered them into the living room, where two women were sitting with a cup of tea. The minister was sitting in a chair, no tea evident. Goode had lived with his sister, and Craig guessed she was the one with the red eyes and sniffles.

'Ms Goode,' Craig said, thinking back to the text from Max he'd read in the car: *Lives with sister. She's unmarried. Has same last name. First name Helen.*

'Yes.' She was fiddling with a hanky as she looked at him.

He turned his attention to the other woman. 'Mrs...?'

'Baxter. Bonnie Baxter. I live next door.'

The minister stood up. He was taller than Craig and had a look about him, like he'd been a boxer at one time and was now squaring up to Craig. He was in his mid-forties, Craig would have guessed if somebody asked him.

'Reverend Josh Fraser. Pleased to meet you.' He held out a hand for Craig to shake, and the detective automatically put one finger along the minister's wrist.

'DCI James Craig. DS Isla McGregor.'

Fraser let go of Craig's hand, his attention now seeking out Isla. He reached out for her hand too and she shook it.

'Pleased to meet you, detectives. I'm here to console Ms Goode at this tragic time.'

Craig looked at the neighbour. 'Would you mind giving us some privacy with Ms Goode? You can make another cuppa in the kitchen with PC Edwards.'

Bonnie stood up and left the room, following Edwards along to the kitchen, where Craig heard her chattering with the officer.

'I'd like the reverend to stay,' Helen said.

Fraser gave her a tight smile. 'Of course I'll stay, Helen. I'm always here for you, you know that.' He looked at Craig, daring the detective to argue with a man of the cloth.

'Please. As you were,' Craig said, shutting the living room door. 'Do you mind if we have a seat?' he asked.

'Go ahead.'

He and Isla sat down on the settee where Bonnie had been sitting, Craig getting the warm spot.

'Do you mind if we call you Helen?' he asked Ms Goode.

'Not at all.'

Craig nodded. Unike the Gregorys' house, this home was neat and tidy. Helen's TV was smaller than the Gregorys', though. Probably not nicked, either.

'I know you've already spoken to one of my colleagues, DI Hold, but I'd like to go over things too, if you don't mind.'

'Anything, if it helps you find out who killed Richard,' Fraser said. 'Helen?'

'Of course,' Helen said, as if she hadn't noticed the look that passed between detective and reverend.

'I'd like you to give me some background on Richard. Like, was he associated with the Gateway Hotel?'

Helen looked at him, and Craig studied her. She

was in her late forties with the beginnings of crow's feet at the edges of her eyes. Her hair was coloured blonde and well looked after. He imagined she might have a nice smile, on better days.

'He worked at the hotel twenty-odd years ago, when he first left the force,' she said. 'A friend of his owned it. He worked in the kitchen. That was before he decided to go back to uni to become a nurse.'

'We also heard about his son, Robert.'

Helen nodded and tightened her lips, pressing them firmly together as if she was going to burst out crying. Then she swallowed and that seemed to release her lips.

'Always playing with fire, that boy,' she said. 'Always playing with matches when he was little. I was shocked when he died, but I was even more shocked before that when he told his father he was at the hotel when it caught fire a few years ago. Then he died in a fire in an abandoned house.'

'What happened there exactly?'

Helen shook her head. 'Always trying to find somewhere to smoke weed. He wanted to smoke in the house, but Richard said no. Especially once he started going out with somebody. Apparently, Robert found the old, abandoned house with his friend and they started smoking weed there. Somehow, the house caught fire and burnt down to the ground. He and his friend died.'

'You said Richard started going out with somebody,' Isla said. 'Was he still seeing her?'

'Oh no, she died,' Helen said. Her lips started trembling and she looked at Fraser.

Craig sat up a bit straighter. Richard Goode didn't appear to have had much luck in his life. 'How long ago was this?'

'Let me see,' Fraser said. He started counting on his fingers. 'Back in the winter. About eight months ago, give or take.'

'Can you tell us what happened?' Isla asked Helen, expecting the woman to say Goode's wife had died in a fire.

Once again, it was Fraser to the rescue. 'She drowned. Just along the road. Richard works... worked...in the nursing home just off the main road in the village, and they had a dog. Kathy was walking the dog one night when Richard was finishing a back-shift, and when he got out of work, Kathy wasn't there. A friend of his was walking by, and he said the police were at the boat ramp that led down into the river and that they had hold of a wee dog like Richard's. When he got there, somebody said the dog was standing barking on the ramp, but there was no sign of Kathy.'

'Did they find her right away?' Craig asked.

'No, DCI Craig. She was found a distance away, two days later. There was a little bit in the paper about it, but not much. If it's not about some overpaid, drugged-up, poor excuse for a human being celebrity shoving something up her...self, the media are not interested.'

Craig didn't have any interest in celebrities, arsehole shoving or not. A thought occurred to him then, something dancing around the periphery of his mind. 'Is she buried here in Newburgh?'

'No, she's buried along the road in Abernethy. It's a small place, no bigger than the size of a playground. Opposite the garden centre. Do you know it?' Fraser said.

Craig shook his head. 'No. I'm not familiar with it.'

'Kathy came from there, you see, and it was her wish to be buried near her parents. I did the eulogy. Performed the service,' he added, as if Craig hadn't got it first time.

'How was Richard after that?' Isla asked.

Fraser looked at her. 'As you would expect any

man to be after losing his wife: distraught. Especially given that he'd already lost his son, in a fire.'

'A preventable death,' Helen said, dabbing at her eyes.

'A preventable death,' Fraser said. 'The boy was obsessed with setting fire to things. First the hotel, then the old house. It was the drugs, see? Prescription drugs can get hold of you.'

'He was over that, Reverend. He was smoking that weed as a way of de-stressing.'

'I can't argue with that, Helen. Probably started the fire to keep warm. Him and that friend of his. Lives wasted,' Fraser said.

They chatted for a few more minutes, then Craig stood up, followed by Isla.

'If there's anything else you think we might be interested in, please give me a call.' He handed Helen a business card. 'We'll see ourselves out.'

They were out of the front door when Fraser appeared.

'I hope I'm not speaking out of turn, and I don't believe I'm going behind Helen's back when I say this, but Richard was troubled.'

'In what way?' Craig asked, feeling the cold running down the hills at them.

'Somebody was always on his back. Getting very nasty, he said.'

'Do you know who?'

Fraser nodded. 'I don't want to speak out of turn, but...' He chewed his bottom lip for a second. 'Seeing as how Richard is dead, murdered, well, I feel it's my duty to let you know.'

'You can tell me,' Craig said.

'It's the undertaker. At the funeral parlour that Richard used when Kathy died. He owns the place, and I've worked with him for a long time, and God forgive me for saying this, but he's not a nice man.'

Craig waited for the name.

'Bruce Campbell. Richard was having trouble paying off the funeral costs. Campbell has burial plans, you see, where you can pay in advance, but after the funeral was paid for using the plan, Campbell told Richard there was a shortfall. Things had got way more expensive. He told Richard he owed more money. Two thousand pounds. Richard didn't have that kind of money, so he told Campbell to go away.'

'And Richard told you this?' Isla said.

'Oh yes. I make house calls. Richard was on lates. So he asked me in for a wee nip, just to chase the cold away, before he had to go to work. Then we got on to Kathy and Campbell again. This had been going on for a long time. Richard said he was starting to get worried that Campbell might do something.'

'Where is this funeral parlour?' Craig asked.

'Along the road, in Abernethy. Small place, but he does a lot of work up here. Like he needs the money. Sorry, I shouldn't be speaking out of turn, but if you'd seen Richard, you wouldn't want Campbell on your Christmas card list.'

'Let me give you my card –' Craig started to say, but Fraser smiled and waved him away.

'I can get your number from the card you gave to Helen. No need for more trees to be felled just to make more business cards.' He stepped back and closed the door.

Isla got in the driver's seat again and Craig slipped in, turning the heated seat on through the entertainment screen.

He looked at his watch. 'We need to head back. I have a meeting in Kirkcaldy at four.'

'I'll give it the biscuit when we hit the motorway.'

'You'll stick to the speed limit, Sergeant.'

'Don't blame me if you're late for your meeting, then.' She pulled out from Abbey Road onto the main street, driving like an old woman driving to church on a Sunday.

'Right, point taken. Get the boot down.'

Isla grinned and sped up, but kept the car at a safe speed.

Then Craig's phone rang. The call went through the car until he directed it to his phone only. 'Hello?'

'Jimmy. It's Duncan. Your brother.'

'Aye, I figured it was my brother since your ugly mug came up on my phone. How's things?'

'I need to talk to you, Jimmy.'

Craig's brows furrowed. He could hear his brother's voice breaking. 'What's up, pal?'

'I need to talk to you, Jimmy.'

'This weekend?'

'I was thinking today. If you could manage.'

'I'm meeting Eve at the Kirkcaldy Galleries at four. We could have a coffee there before she turns up.'

'Fine. Thanks, pal. See you there.'

He hung up, and Craig thought about Richard Goode and a funeral director with a possible bent for violence.

TEN

Glasgow

DCI Angie Fisher sat in the incident room at one of the computers. Robbie Evans and Hamish Connor were at their own computers. Angie spun back and forth on the office chair, alternating between trying to break her teeth with a pen and chewing on it.

Two names were on the screen. Carla Hopper. Collapsed while visiting her boyfriend in Glasgow. Died on the operating table. Originally from Lochgelly, Fife. Dennis Halloran. Local thug. Arrested for beating up a previous girlfriend. Lived in Glasgow. Stabbed to death, probably at the abandoned care home, before having petrol poured over him. Same with Carla. Petrol poured over her and set alight.

Nobody was ever caught. Nobody knew where Carla's body had been taken from. An undertaker from Fife had come down and transported the body back home after the young woman died in the hospital. Her grave was looked at, but there was nothing amiss. Still, Angie knew that it had taken a while to identify her, so of course the grave would have looked undisturbed.

'How's things going?' DCI Jimmy Dunbar said, standing at Angie's shoulder.

'Jesus, Jimmy. I think I peed a little there.'

'That's the usual reaction I get when first introducing myself to a woman.'

'Because you're flashing your warrant card?'

'Yeah, let's go with that.' Dunbar sat on the edge of her desk. 'You making any headway with the cold case?'

'I've been reading through the reports, but the case went cold. Carla Hopper's body was taken to the funeral parlour in Fife, and they had the funeral and then she was buried in Lochgelly.'

'Give Jimmy Craig a call and have him look into it. If it sounds like their case up there, maybe there's a connection.'

'I'll do that. I'll go and have a talk with the parents, listed here as next of kin. I'll have one of Jimmy's team come with me. Maybe Max himself if he's free.'

'Do that.'

'It'll have to be tomorrow or Monday now. I have some work to finish for Lynn.' DCS Lynn McKenzie.

'Meantime, I can have somebody do some digging on the side.'

'Who?'

'Our friend Robbie is married to a private investigator, remember?'

Angie smiled. 'Of course.'

Dunbar turned to Evans. 'Robbie? Got a minute?'

'Sure, boss.' He stood up from his desk and walked over. 'How can I help?'

'You still in your wife's good books?'

'I'm always in Vern's good books.' Evans grinned.

'Poor naive laddie. But do you think she and Muckle would be interested in talking with somebody? As a favour to me.' Muckle McInsh was a former DI with the team and now ran his own PI business.

'I'm sure they would be happy to help out.'

'Are you up to anything tonight? And I mean socially.'

'Watching a film, popcorn on the couch, few beers,' Evans said.

Dunbar nodded. 'You could delay that for a couple of hours?'

'Aye. No bother.'

'Give her a call, son. Angie wants to talk to her.'

Evans took his phone out and called his wife. Handed the phone over after he'd talked to her.

ELEVEN

Craig was aware that he had to meet Eve, so he and Isla left Newburgh and headed back to HQ. The journey would take twenty-five minutes, but they added another fifteen for a stop at Starbucks at Queensway in Glenrothes. Craig was feeling more human now but still needed a refuel.

'A gamer, eh?' he said to Isla when they were back in the car.

'Not going to let that go, are you?' Isla said, settling in behind the wheel again.

'Nope,' Craig said, sipping his coffee through the slot in the cup.

'There are plenty of women and girls who play online games,' Isla replied, starting the engine and taking a sip of her coffee before putting her seatbelt on.

'I'm not slagging it off. I just didn't imagine you doing it.'

She laughed. 'You thought I sat around playing with my cat and knitting jumpers?'

'Of course not.'

'Then what did you think I did in my spare time?'

'To be honest, I didn't give it any thought.'

'Well, now you know.'

Craig laughed. 'I'm glad you enjoy it. I wish I had the manual dexterity to use those game controllers.'

Back at the station, Max Hold was standing at the whiteboard. More photos had been added.

'Who have we got here?' Craig asked, pointing.

'Carla Hopper and Dennis Halloran.'

'Who are they when they're at home?' Craig said. He kept his overcoat on – no point in taking it off as he'd be leaving in a minute.

'They died in similar circumstances to the victims we found today.'

'Whereabouts?'

'Glasgow. I called through to Helen Street and spoke with DCI Angie Fisher. I'd looked through our system, and that case came up. And another one in Edinburgh. I put a call through to them too, and I'm waiting for them to get back to me.'

'I'm sure they're busy. Harry's team will get back to you,' Craig said.

'Yeah, no problem. But anyway, Angie Fisher dug deeper into their case. It's still unsolved. A young woman died in Glasgow. On the operating table, when she had a ruptured spleen. She was brought back to Fife and buried in Lochgelly. Somebody took her. Whether from the grave or before her coffin was buried, we don't know yet. Then she ended up in an old nursing home with a man who was stabbed to death, and then petrol was poured over them both and they were set on fire. DCI Fisher is going to come up tomorrow. She asked if I would go with her to meet the young woman's family if I'm available. Unless you want to do it, sir?'

'Why don't we both meet her, Max?'

'Fine by me, sir.'

Craig looked at his watch. 'I have to go, but we'll talk more tonight.'

'Looking forward to it.'

He turned to Jessie. 'See you at the golf club tonight, young lady.'

'I'll be there with bells on, sir.' Jessie smiled at him.

Craig looked at Isla. 'You got something for me?'

'A smile as you leave?'

'Car keys.'

'I knew that.' Isla fished them out and tossed them to him. He caught them one-handed.

'I get to drive next week, don't I?'

'You get to drive tonight,' Craig said.

'Nice try.'

TWELVE

London

The Red Crown pub was near the police station and was regularly filled with coppers from all departments. Friday night was always jumping after the officers got off work and suits joined the other suits, wannabe hard men rubbing shoulders with the real hard men. And women.

Leanne had always regarded herself as hard. Able to look after herself from a young age, she had never backed down from a fight in her life. But Herman had rattled her cage.

He had been pleasant and funny and charming when she met him. A crime writer and true-crime podcaster, he had made her laugh. Taken her away from the everyday stresses of being a real detective.

Then one evening, he had let the mask slip. A waiter had spilled some water down his back, and he had jumped up and threatened the man. His expression wasn't one she recognised, filled with hatred and violent intent.

She had told him it was fine, they would just go home after their meal and he could change.

'I'll change the way he fucking looks,' Herman said, and Leanne felt a chill run down her back, something that had never happened with a man.

Things had gone downhill after that. There was a shift in their relationship that she couldn't repair. Or didn't want to.

She had called it quits with Herman a week after the restaurant incident.

'Why?' he had asked her.

'I see enough violence at work. I don't need to meet it after work,' she had told him, expecting him to plead with her, and she had an answer ready for him. But he didn't plead.

'Fuck you then,' he told her. 'I wish I hadn't wasted my fucking time with a spoiled little fuck like you.'

She had told him in a coffee house, not wanting

to risk telling him in her flat, in case he didn't want to leave and then she would have to hurt him.

He had stood up, put his jacket on and casually finished his coffee. Leanne was preparing to hurt him from her seated position, but the need to punch him in the balls and then jump up and put his lights out didn't materialise. His next words shocked her more than his fists ever could.

'I'm glad your fucking mother was murdered,' he said, then he laughed. 'It gives me more material.'

He had walked out of her life then and she hadn't seen him since. She had never told him about the postcards when he was her boyfriend. She'd had five sent to her by then. Three months had gone by since that day in the coffee house, and she was always on her guard. Watching for Herman and the man who had killed her mother.

Her father had stood beside her at her mother's funeral. He and Sonia had never been married – at Sonia's insistence! – but he had kept in touch with Leanne all her life, while she was growing up as a little girl, into her teenage years and beyond. It was a relationship she had got used to, and she felt he was her safety net.

Yet she hadn't told him about the postcards. He would have gone mad, insisted on talking with the top brass in her job, and generally made an arse of himself as he had gone into protective mode. And he would have smacked Herman hard.

Now Leanne felt she needed him more than ever, the dad she had always loved but hadn't grown up with.

'That's twice today you've looked like you were on your own planet,' DCI Mike Lewis said, coming up to her with two glasses. Lager for him, vodka and Coke for her.

'Cheers, boss. Sorry. Just reflecting.'

'Don't apologise,' Lewis replied, laughing. 'And it's not boss anymore, remember? Talking of bosses, the missus wanted to come along and have a couple with you.'

She smiled. She reckoned Mrs Lewis was a lucky woman to have Mike in her life. Leanne always felt comfortable in his company, and although he was firm at times, he was always fair. He had taken her under his wing when she joined MIT.

'I forgot,' she said. 'And I'm glad Muriel's coming along. She'll be able to keep you all in check.'

'We're going to miss you, Leanne. If some of those slackers worked half as much as you, the crime rate would drop overnight.'

Leanne laughed. 'Stop blowing smoke through your arse. Sir.'

Lewis patted his jacket pocket. 'Talking of smoking, I was just checking my ciggies are still there. Before you were born, we could smoke in places like these. Until the smoking Nazis got it all banned.'

'I'm twenty-eight, Mike. It was banned after I was born.'

'Yeah, but you weren't smoking when you were a toddler, so it doesn't count.'

'Hey, Leanne, all the best to you,' one of the other detectives said, handing her a drink.

'Cheers.' She raised her glass to him. Then turned back to Lewis. 'I don't want to have too many. I'm driving.'

'No, you're not. You sold your car, remember?'

A woman sidled up to Lewis. 'She means she doesn't want to be seen tossing her load in the lav,' Muriel Lewis said. 'Don't listen to him, sweetheart.'

'I just want the girl to enjoy herself,' Lewis said.

'She can enjoy herself without puking her guts up. Now, I'm your wife and I don't have a drink in my hand.'

'I'll get you one right now, love.' Lewis was moving to go to the bar when a younger man bumped into him.

'Clumsy bastard,' Lewis said as some of his lager sloshed over the top of his glass.

'Sorry, boss. Let me buy you another.'

Muriel turned to the man. 'It's okay, son. No harm done.'

The man smiled at her and walked away.

'Why did you do that?' Lewis complained. 'I was going to fucking lamp him one.'

'Language in front of the ladies. And that's exactly why I stopped you. You don't want young Leanne's last memory of you to be you getting decked by a young Turk.'

'Turk? Fanny, more like. Besides, I have a whole crew behind me.'

'Let's just have a good night. And that drink won't pour itself,' Muriel said.

'Yes, love.'

Leanne looked at the man, who looked like a young Richard Gere. He turned round and smiled at her as he continued walking away. Another time, another place.

'I don't want my husband getting arrested for a bar brawl, whether he's here with his pals or not,' Muriel said.

'Good idea. Here, let me get this round, Mike,' Leanne said as her old boss put his hand in his pocket. Her hand touched something strange in her front pocket where she kept the small purse with her money in it. Something alien that wasn't hers.

She pulled it out and looked at it. A postcard. Touristy London, showing the Houses of Parliament, a double-decker bus, a red telephone box and the wheel. Just like the others.

'Christ, Mike, it's a postcard.' She quickly flipped it over and read the words that were written there. *It's not goodbye. Just au revoir. The Traveller.*

'Fuck me,' Lewis said, forgetting his wife's warning about using foul language. 'Sean'

DI Cargill whipped his head round to look at the boss, knowing something was wrong.

'Boss?' he said, putting his glass down and grabbing hold of one of the sergeants, Roy West.

'The Traveller!' Mike said, his voice urgent but not shouting across the length of the pub.

Cargill and West shoved through the crowd.

'Young bloke just put a postcard in Leanne's pocket. He left through the side door. Black jacket and black jeans. Short, dark hair.'

Leanne ran after the two detectives, followed by Lewis. Outside, the air was cold and dark, the orange sodium lights throwing their glow over the street.

'There's the bastard,' Mike Lewis said, deliberately not shouting. Nobody else gave a shout either, like on TV where the cop will call out, giving the guy a chance to run.

'You're the youngest, Roy,' Lewis said. 'Go get the fucker.'

West had done cross-country running at school and was off like a hare, followed by Leanne and Cargill, Lewis bringing up the rear. The DCI was doing his best but didn't want to puke his drink back up when they got to the young man.

Unlike in the TV shows, the young man who had put the postcard in Leanne's pocket didn't see it coming. Roy West grabbed him and slammed him against a brick wall, and as the man started to struggle, Cargill was all over him, and along with Leanne, managed to get him on the ground.

'What the fuck?' the man said, starting to lash out.

Lewis stepped up, out of breath, and stepped on the man's bollocks in the fray, accidentally. The man let out a scream.

'You stood on my nuts!' he yelled. 'You all saw that!'

'We saw fuck all,' Cargill said, looking at West.

'Fuck all,' West said.

'Fuck all,' Leanne confirmed.

'Bastards.'

'What's your name?' Lewis asked.

'Go fuck yourself.'

'Really? I've heard that name before.' He reached into the man's pocket and took his wallet out. 'Well, Mr Go Fuck Yourself, I see you go by the alias of –'

'I don't give you permission to go through my wallet.'

'Shut it. Where a crime has been committed, namely assaulting a police officer, I have the right to search a suspect.' He looked at the driving licence. 'AKA Curtis Hogarth. People call you Dick? I bet they do. Bit of an ugly bastard in your photo, aren't you?'

'Screw you.'

A few minutes later, a couple of patrol cars swooped in, the officers alerted by other detectives in the pub.

Lewis looked at the man. 'I'm arresting you for assaulting a police officer. That's for starters. By the time we're finished, we'll have hiked the charges up to murder.'

'What are you talking about?' the man said,

squirming. 'The guy paid me money to put that postcard in her pocket. That's all.'

'What guy?' Lewis asked.

'I don't know. Some scruffy bastard. Fifty quid to slip it in her pocket.'

Lewis looked across the road as the young man was held in place by the two uniforms. He saw his wife speed-walking towards him.

He was impressed that she wasn't out of breath, but then she did take care of herself. Unlike Lewis, who drank too much, ate too much shite and sat watching TV too much.

She had her phone out. 'As soon as I saw Leanne take the postcard out of her pocket, I took my phone out and started taking photos.' She showed him. She had lifted her phone above shoulder height and taken rapid-fire photos.

'Good job. Let me see your phone for a minute.'

She handed it over and Lewis put the screen in front of Hogarth. 'Point him out.'

'Who?'

'Don't be a smartarse. By the time you go to court, you'll be more famous than Lord Lucan. You're looking at the judge throwing away the key,' Lewis said.

'I didn't kill anybody.'

'My arm's getting tired holding up this fucking phone. When I put it down, time's up. Point the fucker out, if he even exists.'

Hogarth tutted. 'If these guys can let my arms go, I can point. I can't do Morse code with my eyes.'

'One of you let an arm go,' Lewis said. 'Right arm.'

The uniform let Hogarth's arm go, and the young man looked at the phone and then swiped to the next photo. Three in, he pointed. 'There! That's the bastard. If I'd known what fucking trouble this was going to cause, I wouldn't have bothered.'

Lewis moved the phone, still pointing towards Hogarth. 'Point him out.'

'There. That ugly bastard with the beard.'

Lewis looked at the phone. He remembered seeing the man and thinking there was something odd about him, but in London nowadays that wasn't unusual.

'What did he say to you?'

'He said, "Put the card in that girl's pocket. I'll give you fifty pounds. It's a prank. I'll be watching."'

'Accent?'

Hogarth shrugged. 'London. Well-spoken. Not like you.'

'Don't push your luck.' Lewis looked at the

uniforms. 'Let him go. And you, Hogarth, think yourself lucky I'm not charging you.'

Hogarth shrugged his other arm free. 'See? I told you this was all made-up shit.'

'I can make it assault with a deadly weapon. We carry knives. One of us will wipe theirs down and make sure your prints are on it,' Lewis said.

Hogarth made eye contact. 'Fine. Can I have my licence back?'

Lewis held it out for Cargill to see. The DI took his phone out and took a photo of it. 'There. Now we know where you live. Now fuck off.'

Lewis handed Hogarth his licence and the man skulked away into the darkness.

Lewis showed the photo to the uniforms. 'Give me your number,' he said to the oldest one. 'I'll send you this photo. Get it circulated. Then have patrol get some cars round this area, see if you can see him. It's a long shot, but you never know. He might have stayed around to watch the fun.'

'Or he could have just jumped on a bus,' Leanne said.

'Or the Tube. Taxi. Started running down a side street.'

'Electric bike or scooter,' Cargill chipped in. 'We get the idea, Roy.'

Lewis looked at Leanne. 'How about coming back to our place for a cuppa?' He looked at Muriel.

'Of course, luvvie, you come home with us.'

Lewis handed his wife her phone. 'At least you went out with a bang,' he said to Leanne.

THIRTEEN

'Already dead, you say?' Duncan Craig said.

Craig nodded to his brother. 'Like I said, just keep it to yourself.'

They were sitting in Café Wemyss in the Kirkcaldy Galleries, coffees in front of them.

'Aye, of course. I just said so, didn't I?' Duncan sipped his coffee.

Craig nodded. 'Some things are worth repeating.'

Duncan looked at him and smiled. 'You say that like I'm going senile, Jimmy boy.'

'You are getting on a bit. I just wanted to make sure.'

'Cheeky bastard.' He made a face and tutted. 'Tell me more about this case.'

'We don't know how long the woman's been

dead. The man on the floor likely died within twenty-four hours.'

Craig looked at his brother. Sixteen years older than Craig, but Duncan told him he didn't feel that much older. They were technically half-brothers, but Craig felt a bond with both Duncan and his other half-brother, Callum. Duncan had been in the police and retired years ago; he had been in the traffic department and had loved it. He still liked to keep up with things that were going on in the force.

'That's a queer one, alright,' Duncan said.

'I'm not sure why the killer would dig up a female and then kill a man and place them both at the scene.'

'Screw loose, obviously.'

'He's certainly not firing on all cylinders.'

'I wonder why he chose a man to kill but wanted a woman who was already dead?' Duncan mused. He was drinking an Americano and felt the caffeine taking control.

'We're trying to identify the woman just now, but where do we start? She's been dead a long time, but was obviously embalmed after the postmortem, so she's reasonably preserved. If we can nail down an identity, we can find out where she was taken from and why he chose her.'

Duncan stood up and nodded to the cups. 'Refill?'

'Aye. Cheers. Same again.'

'Righty-ho.'

Craig watched his brother walk towards the counter and felt a love for him that he hadn't felt growing up, mainly because he hadn't met his brothers until he was ten, and then only intermittently until they were young men. Just before Craig headed south to join the Met.

His other brother, Callum Craig, was younger than Duncan and eleven years older than Craig. Callum had distanced himself from Craig recently, since Craig had come back up to Scotland to live. He was the brother who blamed Craig for their father's death, even though Craig had had nothing to do with it.

Duncan came back with the two cups, expertly landing them on the table. 'You look like you lost a pound and found a penny,' he said, grinning and sitting down.

'A case is never far away from my thoughts, Duncan. Whether we're working on a review case or a live one, there's always something kicking away in the back of my mind.'

'I thought it might have been Eve.' Duncan took

a sip of his heart attack in a cup and looked his brother in the eye.

'If that's supposed to make me feel guilty, it's not working. Besides, she'll be here soon.'

'What does she want to talk about?'

'I don't know. Maybe she wants to tell me she fucked up and wants me back.'

'It happens in a marriage, Jim. One half makes a mistake, realises it and wants to go back home.'

'Too much water under the bridge for that to happen. When we found out that our adopted son was a serial killer, it divided us. We thought he was going to uni up here; we had no idea he'd jacked it in and was killing people.'

'Aye, that's a hard pill to swallow, right enough.'

Craig sipped his coffee. 'What did you want to talk to me about?'

Duncan sipped his own coffee before putting the mug down. Looked his brother in the eye. 'I have cancer.'

At first, Craig thought he'd misheard his brother. 'What?'

Duncan nodded. His hand was shaking a little bit as he drank more coffee. 'I've been for the tests. It started with a lump in my neck. I was going to ignore it as it went away. But my doctor insisted I go for a

CT scan. Then, an ultrasound and, finally, a needle biopsy. Then came the phone call telling me it was cancer. It's my Thyroid. I'll need it completely removed. But it's Papillary cancer, the easiest to treat.'

'Jesus, Duncan. I'm so sorry.'

The older man looked at Craig for a moment, his eyes wet. 'It makes you think about mortality. I have to keep the faith, though, Jim.'

'You do, Duncan. I'll be there for you, pal.'

'I appreciate that. The girls will help too, but it might not be easy for them to get off work.' Duncan stared into his coffee for a few seconds, seeing something that only he could see in the brown liquid. Then he looked back at his brother. 'This is when I miss Jean the most. I go to her grave and I have a wee chat with her sometimes, and I went today and told her about the cancer. And you know what? It made me feel better. At least if I go, she'll be waiting for me.'

'Don't talk like that, Duncan.'

'It's true, though.'

Craig looked at his watch. 'I'm going to move to another table and get two coffees. You want another one?'

'With my bladder? No, thanks. Talking of

which...' Duncan stood as Craig got up, and he headed for the stairs at the back, where the toilets were.

Craig bought two more coffees and sat at another table, and Eve walked in with a minute to spare. She walked over to his table.

'Hello, Jimmy.'

'Eve. I got you a coffee.'

'So I see. Thank you.' She shrugged her jacket off and draped it over the back of her chair and sat down, wrapping her hands around the mug.

'What was it you wanted to talk about?'

Eve had cut her hair and it took years off her, Craig thought. She was wearing black jeans and a sweater that might have doubled as an ugly Christmas one. She looked like she had lost some weight. He looked at her face and wondered for a moment where it had all gone to shite.

'I just wondered if there was any chance at all that we could have a chat about our future. If there was any chance that we could make another go of it.'

Craig looked away, at the paintings on the wall, before finally settling on his soon-to-be ex-wife.

'Correct me if I'm mistaken, but you're the one who chose this for us.'

'I know I did. It was my fault, but I wasn't

thinking straight. I thought we should be near our son.'

'Moving to live near the State Hospital wasn't going to change how Joe was.'

'You can't blame me for loving our son. I know you wrote him off –'

'I didn't write him off-' Craig said, interrupting her. 'I'm a detective, Eve. He was a serial killer. And you slept with the doctor who killed him.'

She sipped her coffee, apparently lost for words for a few seconds. 'I'm sorry. I thought you would come down and join me. I thought you loved me enough to do that.'

'I never stopped loving you, Eve. You tore us apart.' Craig sat back in his chair. Eve looked up.

'I see you brought reinforcements,' she said, nodding to something behind Craig's back. Craig turned to look, to make sure his brother was okay. 'He's here to talk about another matter entirely. He's not here because we were meeting.'

'Hello, Duncan,' Eve said. 'Long time.'

'Hello, Eve,' Duncan replied. He looked at his younger brother. 'Did you tell her?'

Craig shook his head. 'No.'

'Tell me what?' Eve said.

Duncan looked at Craig, not sure how to proceed now. Craig looked at Eve. 'Duncan has cancer.'

Eve sucked in a breath, shocked, and put a hand over her mouth. 'I'm so sorry.' She stood up and gave Duncan a hug. He held her, looking over her shoulder at Craig. Craig slowly nodded, a look of understanding passing between them. Eve had been part of Duncan's life for so long now.

'Thanks for your time, Jimmy,' Eve said, after letting go of Duncan. She grabbed her jacket. 'Nice to see you again, Duncan. Keep me in the loop. I hope all goes well with you.'

She walked out of the Galleries.

Craig stood up. 'Take care, brother. We'll have a pint soon, eh?'

'Yes, we will.'

FOURTEEN

Harvey – real name *not* Harvey – was standing at the window again after taking a trip out. He'd been watching for her, just in case she came home early, but she hadn't, so he'd been the one to make the move.

The Red Crown was your basic shithole London pub, filled with a mixture of drunken office workers and in this case, police from around the corner. He'd been there before, of course, sitting and observing from a corner table with a newspaper in front of him to offer concealment, but they had been so pissed, nobody had noticed he was there. Just another suit enjoying a quiet pint at the end of the day before heading off to...where? Anywhere.

Leanne had looked good, even wearing a suit like

a man. He knew the female officers could hardly wear dresses when they sometimes had to grapple with a suspect. He had watched as the young man with the newly acquired fifty-pound note in his pocket made his way over to Leanne and bumped into her and that clumsy oaf of a boss. Harvey knew there was a fifty-fifty chance the young man would get caught. He'd already had a drink in him, and had he not been quite so full, he might have been able to make his escape.

Harvey had stepped outside and watched with amusement as they took down the young man. Then he had left. He had seen the copper's wife start taking photos and he knew he would be in some if not all of them.

What would they see? Some overweight oaf with a bad haircut and scraggy beard. He wore the fake beer belly like a corset, and the hair was a wig, the beard false. Just like he fooled his temporary landlords, the Sturgeons. He couldn't care less if she described him to the police after he was gone. It wasn't as if she could pick him out of a lineup.

He was back standing at the window with the light out, his binoculars pressed firmly to his face.

Leanne wouldn't be driving, but she wouldn't be walking home either, especially after the episode in the pub. She would be getting dropped off, no doubt, either by a friend or some ride-sharing company. He could stand here watching all night if he had to.

He had asked the old boot downstairs if he could have a sandwich for his dinner, and a cup of milk, to have in his room. She had obliged, and he would make sure he wiped off the fingerprints from the glass and plate and the utensils, just like he had wiped off the pint glass in the pub before putting his gloves on to leave.

Several cars went by and a couple stopped, but it wasn't Leanne. After an hour and a half, a patrol car stopped. And Harvey watched with a smile as his target got out of the car.

FIFTEEN

Leanne thanked the patrol driver. His partner stepped out and held the door open for her.

'It was nice working with you, ma'am, and I wish you all the best in Scotland.' The man was built like a brick shithouse and was originally from Glasgow.

'Thank you, Sam.' She stepped forward and hugged the big, burly police officer. He held on to her for perhaps a second too long, then stepped back.

'I thought that bastard was going to hurt you in the pub tonight.' Sam, a rugby player, gave her a look that said he would have ripped the bastard's arms from their sockets if he'd touched Leanne.

'I was fine, surrounded by all my colleagues.'

'I know you were, ma'am.'

'Call me Leanne. I'm officially no longer working with the Met.'

Sam smiled sheepishly. 'Leanne. Now, the boss said I was to see you into your flat and make sure nobody was in there. Me and that wee tube.'

'Cheeky bastard,' said the sergeant, an older bloke called Andy, but then he grinned. He'd seen Sam fight and the Glaswegian didn't take any prisoners. As it were.

The sergeant turned off the engine and got out. 'DCI Lewis said we have to go up and make sure you're okay.'

'Doctor's orders,' Leanne said, smiling.

'Doctor?' Sam said.

'Figure of speech, son,' Andy said. 'Let's just go.'

As they were walking to the front door, Andy felt the hairs on the back of his neck go up, like they were being watched. He turned round to look, but didn't see anybody.

They took the lift up to the second floor. As they were walking along to Leanne's front door, she stopped so suddenly that Sam bumped into her, shoving her forward, but two hands built like shovels grabbed her shoulders.

'What's wrong?' he asked.

'That suitcase. Outside my door. It's not mine.'

'Let me check it out,' Sam said, brushing past her.

'What if it's a bomb?' she asked.

'Then I'll get my baws blown off,' he said, not missing a beat. He walked up to the suitcase and, in an act that would have made every bomb-squad officer cringe, he kicked it. The case rolled a couple of feet away from her door and Sam picked it up.

'It's light,' he said, shaking it. 'Feels empty. But there's a tag on it.' He looked at the tag, holding it with his other hand. 'It's a message for you, Leanne.'

She and Andy walked forward.

'How did you know it wasn't a bomb?' Andy said.

'They put them in backpacks, don't they? Those nutters.'

'You put an awful lot of faith in that,' Andy said.

Leanne was reading the tag. *A wee present from me, Leanne. Enjoy your new life. The Traveller.* It had a drawing of a little suitcase on it.

'He was here. The Traveller,' she said, taking her keys out.

'Was he now?' Sam said, taking the keys from her and unlocking the door. 'You can wait here if you like, Andy.'

'Just get inside.'

'If he's in here, let him have it,' Sam said.

'You mean, we'll arrest him,' Andy said. He was glad Sam was his patrol partner, as the big Scot had saved his arse on more than one occasion.

'Whatever keeps you off the ledge, mate.' Sam went inside, slapping on lights as he went, Andy close behind. They checked the empty closets and cupboards, but there was nobody inside. Leanne's things had been boxed, ready for the removal firm coming the following day.

Sam closed the curtains in the living room before going to get Leanne. 'Coast is clear.'

She walked in, aware that there would not be a single fingerprint in the place. The tag would be dismissed as a hoax by the boss upstairs. Yet, it had been put at her door by a nut job.

'What are you going to do with it?' Sam asked.

'Leave it here. I'll call the movers in the morning, tell them not to touch it.'

'Is there anywhere else you can go tonight?' Andy asked.

'I think so.' She took her phone out and called a number. 'Muriel? It's Leanne. Is there any way I could stay with you and Mike tonight?'

'Of course, love. There's plenty of room since our Suzy moved out. When will you be round?'

'I have two officers with me now. Mike wanted them to come into my flat to make sure everything was okay. I'm sure Mike could authorise them to drop me off.'

Sam and Andy nodded.

'I'll have the kettle on.'

Leanne had one last look around at her flat, which would be on the market next Monday. 'Thanks, boys. Do you know where DCI Lewis lives?'

'Picked him up many a morning when he's hungover,' Sam said. 'You didn't hear that from me, though.'

Leanne left the flat without looking back.

SIXTEEN

Fife

The golf club was in Dunfermline, not far from where Annie lived. Heather, Craig's dog walker, had taken the dog for the night, as Craig didn't want Finn to be left alone for long. They would be heading back to his place after Jessie's leaving party, but Finn would have shown his displeasure at being left alone by then. Right now, they were getting ready at Annie's place.

'Cheer up,' Annie said as she came into her bedroom and saw Craig standing and looking in the mirror in the en suite bathroom, yet to put his trousers on.

He was wearing a casual shirt, having steadfastly refused to put on a dress shirt and tie. 'I wear one all day, every day,' he had told her. 'Tonight, I'm going casual.' Now he was staring at the mirror as if willing the lines at the sides of his eyes to go away. Or the grey that seemed to be taking over slowly.

'I have some bad news,' Annie said. 'It doesn't get any bigger the longer you stare at it in the mirror.'

He turned to look at her, his eyebrows raised. 'I feel I've just been insulted.'

'Your nose.'

He shook his head. 'You're too short to go on this ride.'

'I'll remind you of that quote later, shall I?' She laughed.

'Duncan has cancer.' He had thought of other ways of telling her, of waiting until tomorrow, but it had been weighing heavily on him, and none of the other ways seemed appropriate.

'What?' The smile left and her eyes widened. 'No! When did you find out?'

'This afternoon when we had coffee at the Galleries.'

'I'm so sorry, Jimmy.' She walked over to him and hugged him as he came out of the bathroom. Then she stepped back and looked him in the eye. 'What type?'

'Thyroid,' Craig said simply. 'Papillary.'

'Thank God,' she said. 'Of all the cancers to get, that's the easiest to take care of. It has a fantastic recovery rate. He'll need to take medicine for the rest of his life to replace the hormones his thyroid won't be producing anymore, but it's just a little pill once a day. Easy surgery too.' She knew she was rambling now and stopped.

'That makes me feel better. I'm sure Duncan told me that too, but I didn't hear much after I heard "cancer".'

'He'll be fine. Recovery is quick too. He'll be tired for a while, but plenty of rest and he'll be right as rain.'

'Thanks for putting my mind at ease,' Craig said.

'Of course. We'll need to go and see him, both of us.' Annie looked at him. 'Has he told Callum?'

'I assume. I haven't heard from Callum for a while.'

'You two need to sit down and have a heart-to-heart.'

Craig looked at her. 'What good would that do? He thinks I'm responsible for our father's death. No words from me are going to change that.'

'Try. Now get your trousers on. The taxi will be here in a minute.'

Neither Craig nor Annie played golf, but they were social members of Pitreavie Golf Club in Dunfermline. As were other members of the team. They'd hired the function room at the club for Jessie's send-off, and Isla had been in charge of decorating the room, along with Gary Menzies, who was there mostly to make up the numbers. He had been out of puff blowing up balloons until Isla told him she had a machine for that.

The room had a banner on one wall with 'Good luck, Jessie!' on it, and balloons had been taped on the walls. Music played in the background, competing with the thrum of conversation from those who had already arrived. A buffet was laid out on a table in the back.

'Look at Mark Baker,' Annie said in a low voice to Craig. 'Dressed up, with a woman standing next to him. I wonder if she charges by the hour?'

'Behave yourself,' Craig said. 'She looks very nice. Come on, let's go over and talk to him. See if we can get him to pull a beamer.'

'Twenty pounds says he'll rein it in,' Annie said.

'Done. I say he'll do it within two minutes.'

They walked over to Baker, who was standing at the bar, drinking a lager. His female companion was holding a glass of something red that might have been wine.

'Det Sup Baker! Glad you could make it, sir,' Craig said, smiling at the man.

'Please, Jim, it's Mark tonight.'

'Mark.'

'Hello, Mark,' Annie said, flashing her best smile. 'Aren't you going to introduce us to your friend?'

A slight flush hit Baker's cheeks.

Craig looked quickly at Annie. *You lose.*

'DCI Jim Craig, pathologist Annie Keller. This is my friend, Jean Cathcart. Jean, these are the two reprobates I told you about.'

Craig ordered a pint, and a glass of vodka and Coke for Annie.

Jean laughed and elbowed Mark in the ribs. 'Always one with a joke.' She held out her hand. 'I'm his girlfriend. And he never said anything of the sort. Pleased to meet you.'

Craig shook her hand first, then Annie. Jean looked to be in her late forties and obviously looked after herself. Her hair was blonde and cut short, but not boy short.

'Where did you two meet?' Annie said, going right for the jugular. Baker had been doing a lot of searching on the net for women and had attracted a bad bunch. One psycho had threatened to kill him if he left her, and it had taken a lot of courage and not an insignificant amount of lying to get her to back off. The last lie had Baker moving to take up a position at the North Pole or close to it.

'In a pub,' Jean said. 'I was having a drink with my friends, and I bumped into Mark. We got chatting and he asked me out. I said no.'

Annie raised her eyebrows. 'Yet, here you are.'

Jean laughed. 'I bumped into him again. Same pub. We got chatting again. He seemed nice, so we agreed to have a coffee. We met in Tim Hortons at the Fife Leisure Park up the road. I liked him, and I told him I wasn't interested in a fling. Long story short, after a few dates, he asked me if we were boyfriend/girlfriend. I said I could get on board with that.'

Baker nodded, confirming her story.

Craig took the drinks from the barman and handed Annie her glass.

'Cheers,' he said and they all raised their glasses.

'I'm pleased for you, boss,' Craig said. 'He's been –' he started to say but saw the very subtle shake of Baker's head. *Fuck.* He'd started, so Jean would be expecting him to finish his sentence. Been what? Depressed? Randy? Desperate?

'What do you do for a living?' Annie asked Jean, jumping in. It was Craig's turn to feel his cheeks burning a little. Maybe Jean would think Craig wasn't all there upstairs and was really the janitor at police HQ. He put his glass up to his mouth and started drinking.

'I own the little café at Perth Airport. Near Scone.'

'Excellent,' Annie said.

'If you're in the area and feel like a coffee, pop in. You're always welcome. I do breakfasts as well. On the house. You don't have to be with Mister Mister here. Any friend of his and all that.'

'That sounds good,' Craig said. 'I'll definitely go out of my way for some free scran.'

'But we're not going to bankrupt her,' Baker said.

'Of course not, boss,' Craig said.

'Don't let them take advantage of you,' Baker said to Jean.

'Nonsense, Mark. A wee breakfast now and again isn't going to break the bank.'

There was a sudden cheer and Craig looked round to see Jessie and some of her friends come in. There was a rendition of 'For She's a Jolly Good Fellow' before Jessie came up to the bar. Craig ordered her a drink.

'Here's to the star of the day,' he said, and they all raised their glass to her.

'Cheers, boss. And the big boss.' She smiled at them.

'This is my girlfriend, Jean,' Baker said.

'Hi, Jean,' Jessie said.

'I hear you're going to Glasgow?' Jean said.

'Going back home. I'll be working with a nice DCI. Angie Fisher.'

'She's coming up tomorrow to talk with Max,' Craig said.

'Is she?' Baker said. 'He didn't mention anything.'

'They're just going over some stuff. They had a similar case to ours two years ago. It went cold, so maybe this will reheat it. Max has been in touch with Angie, and apparently the female victim from their fire had died on the operating table. Burst spleen. She was buried in Lochgelly.'

'Good,' Baker said. 'Make sure Max keeps me in the loop on Monday morning.'

'Will do.'

The rest of the evening went without a hitch. Dancing, eating, giving a speech, Craig praising Jessie's work. He slow-danced with Annie, and the drink helped loosen him up and he kissed her on the dance floor.

Later on, after they said their goodbyes, Craig and Annie got a taxi to Dalgety Bay. A cold wind was coming in off the Forth.

'It seems strange not having the boy meet us at the door,' Craig said, missing his dog.

'You'll see him tomorrow. I miss him too. I'm used to having a big, hairy animal in my life. And Finn too.'

She squealed with laughter as Craig pinched her backside as they stepped over the threshold.

SEVENTEEN

Glasgow

Ex-DI Michael 'Muckle' McInsh wasn't missing his dog, as Sparky was right by his side, sitting with him in the car. Muckle had bought a fish supper and was eating it, giving his boy some chips. Before she left him, his wife would have tutted as he fed the dog, but his German Shepherd was a growing boy.

The dog wouldn't have made it through K9 training, and Muckle had had no inclination to be a dog handler, but he didn't mind having his boy around all the time. They'd been practically inseparable ever since he had started his own PI business.

'Ease up there, son, or you'll have all my fucking fish over the floor. It'll smell like a polis pool car if you do that.'

The big dog ignored him and stood with his front paws on the centre console, back legs on the passenger seat, wagging his tail off. He barked a few times.

'That was in my fucking ear! Sit down.'

Sparky reluctantly sat back down but looked at his master like he was on standby and would give it a good go if Muckle took his eyes off the fish again.

'I thought you didn't like that chippie? The last time I got a fish from there, you spat the chips out.' He shook his head. 'You're a daft dug.'

Sparky barked again.

'Oh, here. Have a couple.' He hand-fed the dog, then wiped his hands on a paper hanky before grabbing more fish. Sparky was hardly accurate when grabbing some food from Muckle and sometimes had Muckle's fingers right in his mouth.

'I hope Vern's getting on okay.' He looked at the clock on the screen. 'She's been in there five minutes. After ten, we've to go in, so get your arse ready in case she calls before that.'

The pub on the south side of Glasgow was rough, the sort of place you went to for a fight and then stuck around for a pint afterwards. Vern Evans – DS Robbie Evans's wife – sat on a bench seat with her eyes on the door. The bench was vinyl, with decorative knife marks on it.

Vern had come in here on her own, knowing that her partner, Muckle, was just outside. Robbie had said he would come along for backup, but Vern had insisted that Muckle and Sparky would be backup enough. Things might get a bit rough, so it was best for him not to be there.

The air was thick with cigarette smoke. Smoking was banned, of course, but apparently the management hadn't got the memo. Nobody cared, nobody would make a phone call, and life rolled past them. People with no hope in their lives just coming along to a place where they could be anonymous.

Vern sat with a half pint of lager, alternating between looking at her phone and the door. Tonight might be a bust; their target might not even show up, even though the intel they had was solid.

The door opened, and Vern looked up. It was her. The woman they were looking for. Abi Stevenson.

Vern waited until the young woman had got her

drink from the bar, had a chat with a couple of people she knew and then sat down. Abi's face looked thin, like she hadn't had a good meal in a long time, and her dark hair was from a bottle. She had a nose ring hanging down, with a row of studs running up her left ear.

Vern texted Muckle, *She's here*, in case he was playing with the dog in the car and hadn't seen Abi come in.

I saw.

Vern stood up and walked over to where the young woman was sitting. 'Abi?'

Abi looked up quickly and saw a strange woman standing there smiling at her. 'Do I know you?'

'Do you mind if I sit down?'

'Free country,' Abi replied, going back to her phone.

Vern sat opposite her. 'I'd like to talk to you for a few minutes, if I could.'

Abi looked at her. 'You're not polis, are you?'

Vern gave a small laugh. 'No, I'm not polis. I'm a private investigator, and in a few moments, my partner is going to come through that door with his German Shepherd, and the man you just texted is going to get a surprise when he comes across to me.'

Abi locked eyes with her. 'You used to be polis.'

'A long time ago.'

'I can get up and walk out of here at any time,' she said.

'You can, and I promise I won't stop you.' From the corner of her eye, Vern saw a man get up from the end of the bar and slowly approach them. At the same time, the bar door opened, and Muckle walked in with Sparky just as the man from the bar got up behind Vern.

Muckle walked up to him. 'Three's a crowd,' he said. Sparky stood with his tongue hanging out, panting.

'Why don't you just fuck off and mind your own business, wee man,' the man said, looking at Muckle with undisguised contempt. He took a step towards him. Sparky's ears pricked up, but he just stood watching.

Muckle was a very big man, but this man was inches taller, and he was much broader.

Although Sparky wasn't trained for police work, an old friend of Muckle's used to train the dogs for the police and he'd given Muckle some pointers for Sparky. 'Get a code word for the dog,' he'd said. 'Make sure he knows that code word means he has to protect you, and never use the word unless you want him to go off his heid.'

'Hey, boy,' Muckle said, 'Dad was at the supermarket today. And guess what he got? Bananas.'

Something clicked in Sparky's head when he heard *bananas*, that Dad was in trouble and he needed to rip somebody's balls off. Snarling, he launched himself at the big man, almost grabbing him by the nuts, but the big man was just that little bit quicker. As he yelled, the other patrons started yelling, and they jumped up onto the bar, the big man included.

'Hey! No dogs allowed in here!' the bar manager shouted.

'I'm sure there are a lot of things not allowed in here, but they still happen.' Muckle slipped Sparky off his lead and the dog's front paws reached up to the level of the bar. The patrons who were standing on it jumped behind it now to stand beside the manager. 'You can come round and clip his lead on him if you like?'

Muckle held out the dog's lead, but there were no takers. The dog's paws dropped to the floor, but he paraded back and forth, barking and snarling.

'As I said,' Vern said to Abi, 'you're free to leave any time.'

Abi looked at the dog, a hint of fear in her eyes.

Vern snapped her fingers and Sparky came

across to her, wagging his tail. 'Sit, baby.' Sparky sat but kept a watchful eye on the group of men behind the bar.

'What is it you want?' Abi said.

'I want you to tell me about Dennis Halloran. Like, who might want to kill him?'

'I answered those questions two years ago. I dated the bastard. He had a heavy hand, especially when he was drinking. He broke my eye socket, and I ended up in hospital. I reported him.'

'I saw the report. It says he was angry with you.'

'Den was angry with the world. He had to be taught a lesson,' Abi said.

'Somebody taught him a lesson. A permanent one.'

'I had an alibi for the night of the fire.' She took a sip of her drink. 'That was some weird shite, killing him and setting the place alight with that young woman in there. I mean, she was already dead, wasn't she?'

'She was. She died in hospital from a ruptured spleen.' Vern looked at Abi. 'You know, a lot of women who are physically abused end up with a ruptured spleen. It's located here, above the stomach, on the left-hand side. The rupture is the result of being punched hard there. Trust me, I saw it more than once when I was in the polis. And Carla already had broken bones that had healed.'

'Jesus. I didn't know.'

'He beat you more than once, didn't he? That's why breaking your eye socket was the last straw. And you did the right thing, reporting him.'

Abi nodded. 'This is my local. He followed me in here one night and started shouting abuse. Phil, the big man who obviously doesn't like big dogs, told Den to get out and not come back. Den squared up to him, but his bottle went. He turned to me and told me I wasn't worth it. I had already moved flats by then.' She reached out a hand to Sparky, who sniffed it and then licked it, his tail swishing on the floor.

'Did you see him again?'

Abi shook her head. 'No. I heard he'd moved on. He was court-ordered to go to group therapy to talk about his violence against women, sitting chatting with a bunch of losers like him. I wanted to tell Carla to get out, but I was afraid of going near her in case Den found out.'

'She came from Fife, did you know that?'

'Only from the paper.' Abi looked at Vern. 'You don't think a member of her family killed Den, do you?'

'There are people in Fife talking to them. I don't

think they would have burned Carla as well as burning Halloran.'

'I can't say I'm not pleased that he died, but I had nothing to do with it. I was just as shocked as everybody else. That poor young woman. But I'll be honest, that bastard got what he deserved. Can I ask you, though: why are you asking about him now?'

'The family just want some closure. They asked us to look into it a bit more since the case went cold with the police.'

Abi nodded. 'Den wasn't a very popular man. I think there would have been a lot of people lining up to kick the shite out of him. Like the boys in here.'

She looked at the men, now standing and having a chat and a drink on the other side of the bar.

'Thanks, Abi. I appreciate you talking to me.' Vern stood up. 'Take care of yourself.'

Sparky stood up and looked at her, wondering if she had his squeaky ball in her pocket.

'As you were, boys,' she said to the men behind the bar.

'Come on, boy,' Muckle said.

Outside, it was cold and a wind had sprung up. Fireworks were being set off in pre-Guy Fawkes celebrations.

'Dennis Halloran lifted his hand to more than

poor Carla Hopper,' Vern said as they walked across to Muckle's car.

'Seems like he was a real fucking scrote,' Muckle said, unlocking the car. 'What was the official cause of death?'

'Ruptured spleen. Apparently, Halloran said that he thought Carla had fallen, hence the injury. But knowing what we know about the bastard, he probably punched her.'

'Somebody took him out, but I don't see it being one of her family,' he said as he got into the car, putting Sparky in the back. He turned the engine on. Vern opened the passenger door and looked in at the seat.

'Was Sparky in the front seat again?' she asked.

'He went off his heid when I got the fish supper. You know what he's like with a fish supper.'

'I'll need to get Robbie to brush me down when I get in.' She tutted as she sat down.

'I'm sure he'll like that,' Muckle said, grinning.

'But back to the point: who would have been pissed off enough at Halloran to kill him? And why bring Carla back to Glasgow and burn her as well?'

'That's a bloody mystery. Especially since Fife have another one.'

'And they're not connected, as far as we know.'

'There has to be a connection somewhere, Vern. They just have to look hard enough.'

He drove away.

EIGHTEEN

The sun was out when Craig finally woke up. He hadn't got tanked the previous night, but he'd enjoyed a fine sample of what the golf club bar had to offer.

They had seen Jessie off, and even Annie had made it through the rest of the evening without calling Baker a bawbag. A good night was had by all.

He stretched an arm across the bed and found it empty. He vaguely remembered coming home with Annie and them fooling around, and then he had drifted off.

He didn't have a headache, which surprised him. His mouth felt dry, though, so he padded through to his en-suite bathroom and gave his teeth a brush.

Then he pulled on some jogging bottoms and a dressing gown.

The rooms were inverted in this big house, with the living room and kitchen on the upper floor. This afforded a view over to the Forth Bridges from the living room. He went upstairs quietly.

'How long have you been up?' he asked Annie, walking over to the couch where she was sitting and reading a newspaper. He bent over to kiss her.

'Mmm, minty. You need to drink more often.'

He smiled at her.

'Just after ten,' she said.

He looked at the clock on the wall. Almost twenty to twelve. 'I meant to get up earlier than this.'

'Why? It's a weekend off. Or it would have been if we hadn't been called to the bodies in the hotel yesterday. We could all do with a lie-in now and again.'

'I feel surprisingly good this morning. I had visions of crawling out of the taxi and having to sleep with my head over the side of the bed so I wouldn't choke on my own vomit.'

'You were remarkably steady on your feet. And I told you drinking a glass of water before bed would help counteract the dry-mouth effect.'

'You did that, Doctor.' He yawned and stretched and scratched and yawned again.

'Why don't you go and shower? It'll help wake you up.'

'I will. Then maybe we could grab a bite to eat.' He saw she was already dressed, casually in jeans and a sweater.

'Let's play it by ear. Heather will be bringing Finn round and he'll need a walk.'

'This was supposed to be our weekend away.'

She smiled at him. 'There will be other weekends.'

He kissed her again and went back downstairs to shower. The water felt good running over him and he stood with both hands against the wall, letting the water hit his back, before standing under it again.

He switched on the TV as he got dressed, feeling much fresher. Then he went back upstairs to join Annie.

'You want to watch a film or something?' he asked, sitting down.

'Oh, Jimmy Craig! What's the "or something"?'

'That would be telling.'

The doorbell rang. Craig groaned and looked at the clock. 'Too early for Finn to be coming back. I've just trudged upstairs. I bet it's that nosy old cow down the road wanting to borrow something again. Could you answer the door and tell her I don't have a spare wig, or whatever it is she's after?'

'No, I'll invite her in for a threesome.' Annie grinned.

'Please don't ever joke like that.' He made vomiting motions, sticking his finger close to his mouth. Annie left the room and went downstairs.

A few minutes later, she came back up, and Craig sensed somebody behind her. He really hoped it wasn't the old neighbour, invited in by Annie.

'It's a young woman. She says she's your new team member.' Annie stood to one side and the young woman stepped forward.

Craig stood up and looked at her for a moment before speaking. 'Hello, Leanne.'

She smiled at him. 'Hello, Dad.'

NINETEEN

DCI Angie Fisher's husband was working on a case, so he was in his office with his colleagues. This made Angie feel less guilty about going to Fife on a Saturday.

Before leaving, though, she was talking to Muckle McInsh in a coffee shop. Dennis Halloran was known for throwing his fists around. It was likely he had killed his girlfriend, Carla Hopper, by punching her and rupturing her spleen. Somebody had wanted him dead, but the fly in the ointment was why Carla would have been taken to the old nursing home and burnt as well.

Some random psycho?

'I don't think so,' Muckle said. 'It doesn't fit with my experience of dealing with psychos on the force.

This was planned, Angie. For what reason, we don't know yet. The team dealing with it hit a brick wall.'

'I'm going up to Fife now to speak with DI Max Hold. I want to speak with Carla's family. I know that they were spoken to before, but maybe they will remember something else if I jog their memory. Or maybe they can shed some light on Dennis Halloran.'

'In my experience, victims tend to clam up. I doubt very much that Carla told them anything,' Muckle said.

'I agree, but it won't do any harm to ask.'

'Go for it.' Muckle finished his coffee and they left the coffee shop.

'What are you doing for the rest of the day?' Angie asked.

'Having a beer with Jimmy Dunbar later on. Nothing much else. I'll take the boy for a walk.'

'You need a woman in your life again.'

'To be honest, I've been chatting with my wife again. I miss her. It's not as if we were cheating on each other. I think she misses me too. I'm hopeful that we can sort stuff out. I miss her. I miss the Beagle too.'

Angie laughed. 'Ah. Now we get down to the nitty-gritty. You miss your other dog.'

'Just don't tell the wife.'

Angie patted him on the arm. 'Good luck. Keep me in the loop. And thanks to you and Vern for your work last night.'

'It was no problem. You should have seen those arseholes jumping over the bar when Sparky got revved up.'

'"Bananas" still the code word?'

'What else?'

They each went their separate ways. Angie jumped into her car and headed out of the city, listening to a playlist on her Spotify account. She took the M8 and then connected with the M9 near Newbridge, went over the Queensferry Crossing, and went up the M90 and connected with the A92. It was a pleasant drive. The dark clouds promised rain, but it held off.

The satnav took her to Fife Division HQ, where Max was waiting. It had been just over an hour since she left Glasgow. Angie was shown to the incident room.

'Good to see you, ma'am,' Max said, holding out his hand.

'It's the weekend, Max. Call me Angie.'

'Angie it is. Can I offer you a coffee?'

'Sure. Black, please.'

Coffees in hand, they went out to Angie's car. She drove, guided by Max.

'Two friends of mine spoke to an ex of Dennis Halloran's last night. He used to throw his weight about with his girlfriends. She reckons he hit Carla and that's how she ruptured her spleen. But we'll never know since she died on the operating table.'

'Men hitting women happens more than you'd think,' Max said.

The quickest way was back down the A92 to the Lochgelly turnoff, then into the outskirts of town and a quick right at the third roundabout.

The cemetery was on the left. Two stone posts marked the entrance, one of which was missing its cap. There was one gate and it was open. Just inside was the caretaker's house, the front door facing them. Angie pulled around the back and parked next to a detached garage, and they got out.

The wind ran at them from the hills in the distance, cutting across the open fields beyond the cemetery.

'Jesus, it's cold here,' Angie said, hunching her shoulders up. 'I should have put on a long overcoat since I was coming to the sticks.'

'You get used to it,' Max said, pulling on his own overcoat.

'I don't suppose there's a chance you would let me have a shot at that coat?' she asked.

'It's too big for you, Angie.'

'Just as well you're a murder squad detective, as it appears chivalry really is dead.'

'I just don't want you to look daft,' Max said, grinning.

'Help you?' a voice said. They turned round to look at him. He was a big man with a beer belly. Unkempt hair, unshaven, hands shoved deep into the pockets of a dirty old jacket.

'Police. Who are you?' Angie said, taking her warrant card out and holding it up in front of her.

'Ed Watkins. I'm the caretaker here. What do you want?' He dug his hands in deeper as Angie and Max approached him.

'DCI Angie Fisher. DI Max Hold. Is there somewhere we can talk?'

'Inside the house. But I can't be long. There's a funeral going on down there, and I have to supervise that pair of lazy twats who have to fill the hole in afterward.'

'That would be fine. It's just a quick word we want.'

'Follow me.'

They followed Watkins back round to the front

door of the house. 'Can't be too careful nowadays,' he said, opening the door. 'Not after what happened.'

They stepped into the warmth of the house, Max bringing up the rear. Angie turned to Max as he stepped over the threshold. 'I hope you sweat in that overcoat,' she said, a smirk on her face.

Max slipped the coat off.

'Bastard,' she whispered.

Watkins disappeared into a room on the left. The living room, as it turned out. Angie was expecting a midden, but it was immaculate.

'The wife's away shopping, but I know my way around a kettle if you want a cuppa,' Watkins said. 'I'm having one. Coffee. I was out with my pals last night and might have had one too many. I bet you thought I was a right scruffy-looking bastard when you first saw me.'

'No, no, not at all,' Max said.

Angie made a face and looked at Watkins. 'I did. Coffee sounds just the ticket. Can we call you Ed?'

'Can I call you Angie and Max?' Watkins looked between the two of them, a smile on his face, like he was playing with them. 'And you're obviously not from around here, but I can tell he is. No offence.' He looked at Max.

'Sure. I'm from Glasgow. Just up for the day,' said Angie. 'I like mine black, thanks.'

'Okay, Angie. You, Max?'

'Little bit of milk, thanks, Ed. No sugar.'

'One black. One milk, no sugar.' Watkins smiled at them and took his jacket off. Much to Angie's relief, he was wearing a sweatshirt underneath. 'Let me take your overcoat, Max. It's not like I can nip out the back and pawn it.' He laughed at his own joke.

'There you go, pal,' Max said, handing his coat over.

'Grab a seat. Just don't take it anywhere,' Watkins said, leaving the room with Max's coat and his own.

Angie and Max sat on a couch facing a big TV. Two leather chairs flanked the couch. An electric fire flickered in the fireplace. A coffee table in front of the couch held a gardening magazine.

Max looked at Angie. 'What? He's right. There are no charity shops near here. Besides, I left nothing in the pockets.'

'Pal?'

'I just want to be friendly with the bloke.'

'If he wasn't married, you could move in with him.'

'You're funny, boss. But my girlfriend might have something to say about that.'

'This is a nice place,' Angie said, looking around. 'For a house in a cemetery. Do you think you could live in a place like this?'

'Absolutely. Quiet neighbours.'

'The solitude would get to me.'

They chatted until Watkins came back with three mugs and put them down on the coffee table.

'Get much gardening done here?' Angie asked, picking up her coffee.

'We do, actually,' Watkins said, sitting down on one of the chairs with his own coffee. 'There's a walled garden at the side of the house. Behind the wall where you parked. The wife loves it. I told her that if she needs more space for gardening, there's plenty spare out there.'

Angie and Max looked at him.

'I'm kidding. This cemetery won't be filled for years. I'll be in there before that happens. But you're not here to talk about me kicking the bucket.'

'No. We're here to ask about Carla Hopper.'

'I knew it!' Watkins said, putting his coffee mug down and pointing at Angie. 'I knew there was something wrong.'

Max was in the middle of taking a sip of coffee

when Watkins had his outburst. He almost sprayed the coffee all over the carpet.

Angie scooted forward on the couch. 'What do you mean?'

Watkins jumped up so suddenly – no mean feat considering his weight – that Max was on his feet in a heartbeat, more throwing the mug onto the coffee table than lowering it. Some of the coffee spilt over the lip onto the table.

'Never mind, son,' Watkins said. 'Come on, let's get your coat. I want to show you something.'

After Watkins handed Max his coat back in the hall, Max put it on and they went back out into the cold.

'You'll have to drive,' Watkins said to Angie. 'Madge has the car. I told her we need another one in case of emergency, but she says that's just wasting money.'

'No problem. Where are we going?'

'Over there,' Watkins said, pointing. 'The funeral is taking place in the new patch, as I call it. We're going to the older patch. It's not the oldest patch, mind. That's way over there.' A nod this time, the hands going back into the jacket pockets, having had enough of the cold.

'I can see what you mean when you say you'll be

pushing up the daisies before they fill this place,' Max said.

Angie looked at him.

'He's right,' Watkins said. 'And when this place is filled, they'll knock the wall down, do a compulsory buy of some of the land next to it and use that. Cremation is killing burials nowadays. It's more convenient, until the government stops that. They'll say the smoke is killing the planet. But that's a whine for another day. Come on, let's get in your motor, and I'll give you directions.'

The burial areas were laid out in squares, the newer ones bigger than the originals. The hearse for today's funeral was on the west side of the south square in the newer part. Funeral cars were behind, followed by mourners' cars.

'I swear to God, I don't know how he's still in business,' Watkins said from the back seat, leaning between the two front seats as far as his big belly would let him.

'Who would that be?' Max asked.

'The funeral director. Bruce Campbell. Arsehole.'

A look passed between Angie and Max: *maybe keep that out of the report further down the road.*

Angie reversed out onto the driveway, the back of the car facing the funeral.

'Look who it isn't,' Watkins said. 'That other glaikit bastard, Josh Fraser.'

Max craned his neck to look at the mourners. 'Which one is he? And why the dislike?'

'He's the minister,' Watkins said. 'Insists we call him Major. He was a padre in the army before he retired. Talks to people like he's still in the fucking army.'

'First the funeral director's a wanker, now the minister?' Angie said. 'What did they do to piss you off?'

'In my own defence, I didn't say he was a wanker. I was just questioning out loud why he's still in business.' Watkins looked between the two detectives. 'He's the one who carried out Carla's funeral.'

'Interesting,' Max said. 'We should talk to him after you show us what it is you've got to show us.'

'Right. Drive straight along and follow the drive as it turns to the left, and go right to the bottom, close to the treeline.'

Angie did as instructed, driving slowly and watching as the gravestones went by, seeming to get older the further they drove, like she was going back in time.

'Stop here!' Watkins shouted as they neared the treeline, throwing himself back in the seat before reaching over to pull the handle to get out. Nothing happened. 'Child lock,' he said sheepishly.

Max got out and opened the door for him as Angie got out the other side.

'Still attached to the overcoat?' she said under her breath as Watkins walked away.

Max grinned at her.

'Bastard,' she said for the second time since they'd got there.

Carla Hopper was buried in the last row opposite the trees, her grave facing the driveway.

'It's an old family plot,' Watkins said. 'Buried next to her grandmother and grandfather. There's a stone waiting for her mother and father. The father had bought a plot for Carla, not imagining it would be used in his lifetime.'

'He told you this?' Angie asked.

Watkins looked from the grave to her and shook his head. 'No. I was earwigging. He told Major Fraser. Big lanky streak of piss.'

'Deary me, Ed,' Max said. 'What way is that to speak about a man of the cloth?'

Watkins snorted. 'It's just his holier-than-thou attitude.'

'He *is* a minister,' Angie offered.

'He's always smiling. Like we're all sinners and he can't help letting us know.'

'You just don't like him, is that it?' Max said.

'Pretty much. I mean, what man spends his years in the army as a chaplain, then comes out into civvy street and starts being a minister out here like he's been doing it all his life?'

'At least he's doing good work,' Angie said.

'I know he is, but he has that smarmy look about him. Still, he seemed to be comforting the family when they had to bury Carla for the second time.' Watkins looked at them. 'As if it wasn't bad enough losing her twice, but I'm convinced she was dug up from here.'

'Okay,' Angie said, 'let's hear what you've got.'

Watkins stomped the ground a couple of times like he was trying to flatten the grass more. 'Two and a half years ago, Carla was buried here for the first time. I supervised the interment. Watched over that pair of bawbags as they filled the grave in. The sod was put back, and it took a wee while to settle. I drive around here every day, just to look out for any problems, like if a gravestone starts leaning.

'A few weeks after the funeral, the ground looked like it had been disturbed. I asked the gravediggers about it, but they said they didn't know anything about it. We hadn't had a burial for weeks, so they hadn't been around. It looked to me like the ground had been dug up and put back again, but my wife said I was imagining it.'

'Then you heard what had happened to Carla?' Angie said.

'Correct. I knew that my instincts were right. Somebody dug her up after the funeral, when it would have been easy to move the sods of grass and then lay them back down.'

'It would have taken a small backhoe like the one the gravediggers use, wouldn't it?' Max said. 'I see the one on the back of the trailer parked near the funeral that's going on just now.'

'It would. That van and trailer with the hoe on it get parked up here at night. When I noticed the grave had been disturbed, I had been in Spain for two weeks. It would have been easy for somebody to come in here and grab the body and put the hoe back.'

Angie shivered in the cold. 'How would they have accessed the machine?'

'The garage wasn't secure back then. There are tools in there and the key to the van, but the gate is locked. We're more secure now, but we're a bit of a walk from town, nobody really knows the garage is unlocked.'

'Somebody did,' Max said.

'Aye. Campbell did. He probably overheard the boys talking about leaving the garage unlocked.'

'How would he have got Carla out of the cemetery?' Angie said. 'He would have needed a vehicle. But he wouldn't have parked outside by the locked gate, I don't think. Too narrow a road. Heavy trucks going by.'

Watkins nodded. 'I thought about that.' He turned and pointed towards the treeline at the side. 'There's a little narrow road that runs parallel to the cemetery. On the other side of the railway tracks. There's an unofficial lay-by where people illegally dump their shite. It's big enough for a car to park. Or a van. He could have parked there after dark, crossed the tracks and slipped into the cemetery that way. Got the key, used the backhoe, dug Carla up, put the dirt back and tried to make it look like it hadn't been touched, and then took her back the way he'd come. Risky but doable.'

'You *have* given this a lot of thought,' Angie said.

'I have. I told somebody from Dunfermline CID, and they said they would come out and have a look, but they never did. Then when she was found weeks later in Glasgow, somebody *did* come out. But you know what?'

Both detectives shook their heads to indicate that they didn't know what.

'Carla had been identified by then using dental records. When her boyfriend was identified, they'd started looking at people who had known him. Her body was brought back here by Campbell, and the grave was dug again. So there was nothing for CID to see.'

'Any idea who could have dug her up?' Angie asked.

'I'm not pointing the finger, but Campbell knows his way around a grave. He obviously met with the family a few times and got to know them. I don't think you'd be far off if you looked into him a bit more.'

Angie and Max turned to look at the undertaker in the distance. Bruce Campbell was looking back at them. As if he knew.

TWENTY

Craig looked between Annie and Leanne. They were all standing in the living room.

'Annie, this is...Leanne is my...'

'Love child,' Annie said.

Craig felt his cheeks burning.

Leanne laughed, and Annie joined in.

'I think your father is a bit uncomfortable,' Annie said. She reached out and squeezed Leanne's hand.

'Detective Chief Superintendent Bill Walker called me after I made the application for a transfer,' Leanne said. 'I came up for the interview, and he wanted to introduce me to Annie, because of your relationship. He said it would be up to me if I wanted to tell her who I was. I did. She's so sweet.'

Craig sat back down, and the two women followed suit.

'I went down to London to look at the possibility of joining the Met, and that's when I met Sonia Chalmers. We had a brief fling, it was a fun summer, and later I found out that she was pregnant,' Craig said to Annie. 'I wanted to be in Leanne's life, but Sonia was a free spirit. She didn't want to be with me but said I could be in Leanne's life. She would even tell her the truth. I made sure Sonia was taken care of financially. Sonia said I should get on with my life. I had just started seeing Eve. It was later on, when I had finished my probation, that we moved to London. I saw Leanne more often then.'

'And Eve never found out about your daughter?' Annie asked.

'Not that I know of,' Craig said.

'I got to see more of Dad when he came to live in London. He helped me get into the police.'

'That was all you,' Craig said. 'You wouldn't have got in if you didn't have what it takes.'

Annie looked at Leanne, then at Craig. 'Leanne told me about what happened to Sonia. Being murdered. I'm so sorry.'

Craig nodded. 'They still haven't got the bastard.'

'I don't want you to think I'm running away from that situation,' Leanne said. 'I just wanted something different. If I didn't get into Fife, I was going to try Glasgow. Then Edinburgh.'

'Bill Walker's a good guy. And he's okay with my daughter working beside me on the team?'

Leanne nodded. 'He is. As long as you aren't going to have a problem with it.'

'I don't have a problem. As long as you understand that I'll treat you as I would any other member of the team.'

'Of course. I wouldn't expect anything less.'

'Jessie Bell, who you're replacing, was a DC, and you're a DS, but you'll be keeping your rank, I assume?'

'DCS Walker said I will.'

'That's good.' Craig looked at his daughter. Twenty-six years old and he could see some of himself in her looks. Then a thought occurred to him: 'Where are you staying?'

She smiled and looked at Annie. 'Your lovely girlfriend has offered to let me stay until I can find a place. My furniture is going into storage, but I have my eye on a property.'

'She already has her bedroom made up,' Annie said.

'You've thought of everything, haven't you?' Craig said.

'Pretty much. Hey, I wasn't going to let your daughter struggle to find a place to live. Besides, it's only for a little while.'

'I appreciate that, but she could have stayed here.'

'Listen, when I stay over here, Leanne will have her own privacy.'

'Fair do's.' Then his mobile phone rang. It was Max.

'I have to take this,' he said, getting up and leaving the living room. 'Max?' he said, going into the kitchen.

'Boss. DCI Angie Fisher and I have been talking to the caretaker here at Lochgelly cemetery. Carla Hopper, the victim from Glasgow who died on the operating table, was buried here. And after she was buried, this caretaker thought her grave had been disturbed.'

'Disturbed? How?'

'Like the earth had been moved and the grass put back. Like she had been dug up from here. Looks like whoever burnt her body and killed Dennis Halloran dug her up and took her from the cemetery.'

'We need to talk to her family.'

'Right. And the caretaker, Ed Watkins, does not like the funeral director from Abernethy. He does a lot of funerals around here. Watkins says Bruce Campbell is dodgy.'

'When I spoke to the reverend, he said that Campbell and our victim from yesterday had had words. Over some financial situation. We can look into him more when we get back to the office. Meantime, I'd like to come along and talk to the family with you and Angie. And I'll bring the newest member of the team.'

'Great. Leanne seems like she'll be an asset. Your daughter has an impressive CV.'

'Christ, is there anybody else who knew about this apart from me?'

'Not for me to say, boss.'

'See you soon.' He hung up and walked back through to the living room. 'How would you like to start two days early?' he asked Leanne.

'Fine.'

'You wouldn't mind if we popped out for a wee while?' he said to Annie.

'That's okay. You two go do what you have to do.'

TWENTY-ONE

Three ways to get to Lochgelly from Dalgety Bay. Craig decided to take the B981.

'Thank you for being so understanding,' Leanne said. 'And I promise I won't call you Dad when we're at work.' She laughed.

'Yeah, that might not go down too well with the team.'

'To be honest, I think Bill Walker only told Mark Baker and Max Hold. About me, I mean.'

'Mark Baker knew too? He was pished last night and still didn't blurt it out. Kudos to him.'

'I hope the others won't be put out when they find out I'm your daughter,' she said.

'Isla is great. She'll take you under her wing.

Gary Menzies is solid. We're a tight-knit team, so you'll be fine.'

'I've never had a problem with team members.'

'You'll fit in just fine.' Up the road through Crossgates. 'I'm assuming you don't have anybody special in your life?' he asked her.

She laughed, a short, bitter laugh, and Craig almost expected her to spit as well. 'Just losers.' She looked at him for a moment. 'I'm also being stalked.'

Craig whipped his head round to look at her.

'Eyes on the road, boss.' She smiled. 'We're at work now, so it's not *Dad*, remember?'

'What do you mean, stalked?'

'We think Mum was murdered by The Traveller, remember?'

'I do.'

'My team got a tip-off and they issued a warrant for his arrest, but he got a call from somebody giving him a heads-up and he scarpered and fell into the river. And we never saw him again.'

'I remember you telling me about that.'

'I've been getting postcards from him.' Leanne didn't look at her father as he drove along in silence for a few moments.

'Did you tell anybody about this?' Craig asked

finally, his veins filled with ice and his head full of thoughts that didn't belong in a police officer's head.

'I did. My superintendent. He said it was a hoax. No fingerprints on them. They tested the first two but not the others.'

'Your boss just shrugged it off?' Craig said, gritting his teeth.

Leanne nodded. 'Yes. My immediate boss, DCI Mike Lewis, has been supportive. He's like a good friend. He and his wife. He was there when the suspect fell into the river.'

'Do you think it's been some kind of elaborate hoax?'

Leanne shook her head. 'When I got home last night, there was a small suitcase waiting for me. With a label on it. Signed "The Traveller". He seems to know all about me.'

'When did you start to get the postcards?'

'About a month after Mum was murdered.'

Through Cowdenbeath now, turning right onto Main Street, heading east towards Lochgelly.

'Tell me, do you think the killer died that night?'

'I don't think he was the killer, so no. I think he was the fall guy. Literally. And now the killer has latched on to me. I have the postcards he sent me. I'll let you read them later.'

'Okay.'

They reached Lochgelly and Craig weaved through the streets, listening to the satnav, until he found a road called The Avenue in the southeast of the town. The housing estate was relatively new, built in the last few years on what had once been just a field.

Craig pulled in behind Angie's car, as described in a text from Max. Craig and Leanne got out, as did Angie and Max.

'Hey, Leanne. Good to see you again!' Max said, walking over and shaking her hand.

'When did you two meet?' Craig asked.

'I was at the mortuary one day, and Leanne was there talking to Annie. Bill Walker took me aside and asked me if I was okay with Leanne coming to work with us. Not that my opinion would have mattered either way, but I'm more than happy. She still has to meet the others.'

'Just treat me as a normal member of the team,' Leanne said.

'Does Isla know?' Craig asked Leanne.

'Maybe,' Leanne said. 'Well, okay, she does, but unofficially.'

Craig nodded. 'And you're DCI Fisher, I'm assuming?' he said.

'Angie.' She smiled and shook both their hands.

'Angie has been a lot of help,' Max said. 'They have a cold case which is exactly the same as our case,' he explained. 'They have to be linked.'

Craig looked at the modern house in front of them. 'One link is here, Fife.'

'Let's go and talk to the family,' Angie suggested. 'Lead the way, Jimmy.'

Craig walked up to the door and before he could knock, it opened.

'It's not every day that a bunch of strangers stand and talk outside my door,' said the man in the doorway. 'Unless it's Jehovah's Witnesses. But they carry clipboards or whatever it is they carry. You must be the police.'

'We are, sir.' They held out their warrant cards. Craig introduced them all.

'Unless you're here collecting for the Christmas party, I'm guessing you're here to talk about my Carla again.'

'You're Carla's father?'

'I am. Robert Hopper.'

'Can we come in?'

'Of course.'

He led them into his living room. 'Please, take a seat.'

Craig took a chair while the other three sat on the couch.

'Can I get you anything?' Hopper asked.

It was a unanimous decision that they didn't want anything. Hopper sat down in the other chair.

The room was clean and tidy, with a large-screen TV sitting in a corner. There was a dresser with family photos on it. One of a woman, a young girl and Hopper himself.

'How can I help you?' Hopper said.

'We believe that Carla was taken from her grave shortly after the funeral and taken away,' Angie said.

'By whom?'

'We don't know that yet. The grave looked like it might have been disturbed, but somebody did a good job of making it look like it hadn't been,' Max said.

'Who would do such a thing?' Hopper asked, his voice catching in his throat.

'That's what we're trying to establish,' Craig said. He looked at the photos again. 'Is Mrs Hopper around?'

Hopper swallowed. 'She died. Suicide. A week after Carla's second funeral.'

'Can I ask you how she died?' Craig asked.

Hopper looked at him for a moment, composing himself. 'She jumped in front of a train, outside the cemetery where Carla's buried. Just along the road. The driver said he didn't see her until the last minute, when she came firing out in front of him.'

'I'm so sorry to hear that,' Angie said.

'The thing is, and I know it sounds crazy when I put it into words, but I don't think she killed herself.'

'What makes you say that, sir?' Leanne said.

'You're English,' Hopper said.

'I am.'

Hopper took a breath and let it out through puckered lips. 'So was Sarah, my wife.' His eyes drifted away for a moment. Then he focused. 'Her mother came up here and brought the family. Sarah and her brother, Tom. He died years ago. Her mother went into a nursing home. The one where Sarah worked.'

'Which home was that?' Craig asked.

'In Newburgh. Carla worked there too, before she went to uni in Glasgow.'

'You wouldn't happen to know if Sarah knew Richard Goode? He was a nurse at the home.'

'Richard? Yes, of course. She didn't like him at all.'

'Why was that?'

'She said he was a useless cretin. Whenever something dirty had to be cleaned up, he'd disappear.

He was useless. And he was always sharp with the patients. How his wife stayed with him, Sarah didn't know.'

'What did Sarah say about his wife?' Craig said, shifting forward in his seat. It was warm in the house and he was starting to sweat a bit.

'Sarah thought that Richard was good with his fists, if you know what I mean. She thought that he used to hit his wife. Goode was always stern with the women in the home. Sarah thought he was a coward. Kathy, his wife, had been married before. Sarah got talking to her on a night out one time. Her husband had died. She missed him, and when Kathy had too much to drink, she confided to Sarah that she wished she was still married to him.'

'Do you know what his name was?' Craig asked. 'Kathy's first husband.'

Hopper made a face, looked away for a second. 'Keith. Kevin. Something like that. Sarah was upset about that. She liked Kathy, and to hear her nice husband had died and then she'd married that lowlife really got to Sarah. She hated Goode. He yelled at her one time when she dropped something, and he walked up to her with his fists balled like he was going to hit her. But the major stepped in.'

'Who?' Craig asked.

'The minister,' Max said, looking to Hopper to see if he would be corrected. He wasn't. Max looked at Craig. 'We saw him earlier, when he was at a funeral just along the road at Lochgelly cemetery. He was a padre in the army. Josh Fraser.'

Craig nodded. 'I met him. In Newburgh. He's a big, imposing guy.'

'Yes, he is,' Hopper said. 'If you take off the dog collar that he wears, you would think he was a bouncer in a nightclub.'

'How well did Sarah know Fraser? Was he at the nursing home a lot?' Max asked.

'Oh yes, he was there all the time. He went around to nursing homes to talk with people who wanted to talk. And to talk to people in group therapy sessions.' Hopper hung his head for a moment. Then he looked at Craig. 'That's where Carla met him. That Halloran man was hitting her. She wouldn't admit it, like a lot of battered women won't, but Sarah knew. I did too. I'm afraid I didn't do anything about it. I have a bad back. Sarah said that was an excuse. She wanted me to take care of Halloran.'

'Take care of him how?' Angie asked. 'Take him to an old, abandoned nursing home and stab him to death? Burn him afterwards?'

Hopper nodded. 'Yes. Pretty much that. At least get in his face. Use my fists. Teach him a lesson. And believe me, I wanted to. But my Sarah was right: I'm useless. I was an accountant working in Edinburgh until the day I fell down a flight of stairs. I messed up one of the discs in my back. I couldn't fight my way through wet toilet paper. I refused to get into a physical tussle with him. I'm not used to fighting. I started my own accountancy firm, and I'm doing quite well with it, but that's all I'll ever be, a desk jockey.'

'Somebody sorted Halloran,' Craig said. 'The mystery is, why dig up your daughter and leave her beside him?'

'I have no idea.'

'What about Goode?' Leanne asked.

'Sarah thought he was only a hard man when it came to women.'

'Do you think he could have done something to Sarah?' Max asked. 'At the cemetery?'

'Pushed her in front of a train? Quite possibly.' Hopper looked at the detectives. 'This doesn't put me in a good light, does it? A man who physically hit my daughter died in a fire after being stabbed. And a man who worked with my wife and could possibly have murdered her died in a fire.'

'It would throw up red flags, yes,' Angie said.

'I didn't kill them. You could ask a medical professional for an opinion on whether I have the physical strength to do it or not. They would tell you that I don't. Besides, if I was going to kill Halloran, I wouldn't have dug my daughter up and left her with that scumbag.'

'Bruce Campbell handled the funeral, didn't he?' Max asked.

'Yes, he did. Another weirdo. I didn't like the man, but Sarah knew him from him coming to the nursing home. She wanted him to do the funeral.'

'Both times?' Craig asked.

'Yes. He's very popular around here. It's been a family business for a very long time. People trust him more than they trust the big conglomerates sometimes.'

'How long has Fraser been the minister around here?' Angie asked.

'I'm not sure. A few years, I think. He retired from the army, is what Sarah said. He did his time, got his pension and now he's a minister in Newburgh, but he floats around. He's like the proverbial bad penny. I don't like either him or Campbell, but Sarah was indifferent.'

'Who arranged the funeral for Sarah?' Craig asked.

Hopper looked down at his carpet for a second before answering. Then he met Craig's eyes. 'Campbell arranged everything. It was Sarah's wishes, what she wanted to happen when she died. I wouldn't give him house room, but I respected my wife's last wishes. You see, Sarah knew him growing up. They grew up together here.'

'I can understand why she would want Campbell to do the funeral,' Craig said, 'if they were friends growing up.'

Hopper nodded. 'Sarah was there for him. After the tragedy. Fraser too. They were all friends.'

'What tragedy?' Angie asked.

'The fire,' Hopper answered.

Craig looked at the man, wanting him to explain in one sentence, not piss about feeding them details, but he also didn't want him to clam up. They waited for him to explain further.

'Campbell's father owned the funeral business at the time. Their house went up in flames. Campbell Senior was a horrible old bastard. Treated Bruce's mother like crap. Apparently, Bruce Campbell tried to save the family but he couldn't. They all perished in the fire. He was distraught.'

'Where was the house?' Angie asked.

'You go through town, heading north. It's up a track. The ruins are still there, apparently.'

'We should talk with this Campbell,' Craig said.

'We saw him doing a funeral at the cemetery,' Max said. 'We can find out where he is now and talk with him.'

'Fraser told me that Campbell still has the business in Abernethy,' Craig said.

'He does. Been there for years,' Hopper confirmed.

They chatted some more and then left the house. Gathered outside again like the Jehovah's Witnesses were undecided what house to hit next.

'I think we should have a drive up to Abernethy. See if we can find this Campbell and have a wee chat,' Craig said.

'Agreed,' Angie said. 'See if we can track down Fraser too. If they're finished at the cemetery, and Ed Watkins seemed to think they would be by now' – she looked at her watch – 'then I'm assuming they would be taking the cars back. If Fraser's not there, Campbell might know where he is.'

'Before we go and talk to him, I'd like to have a look at the house that went on fire years ago. Just to see the place for myself. You want to come along and have a wee neb with me?' he said to the others.

'Absolutely,' Angie said. The others nodded.

'Let's go,' Craig said.

TWENTY-TWO

Isla McGregor hadn't been this excited in a while. Of course, she'd been on dates, but meeting Ian Bark for the first time in person was exciting. He had told her he was staying in Edinburgh and would get a train across to see her. Surprisingly, the mechanic had called her and told her they had managed to finish the work on her car early, so she'd taken an Uber down and picked it up. She could pick Ian up at the train station, and then he would take her for a coffee and they would see how they got on from there.

It had been a while since Isla had been in the company of a man. Even going for a coffee would be a nice change. She looked at herself in the mirror; she was wearing a V-neck sweater and black jeans. Not exactly scaring him away with a polo neck, but not giving anything away either.

She wouldn't invite him back to her place. It would be great to meet him, but she wasn't stupid. Besides, he was just up in Scotland doing some research on a cold case. If she could help him, she would, but she couldn't divulge any behind-the-scenes stuff.

She brushed her hair again. Thought about applying some more make-up but then thought that might give off the wrong signal. They were friends, that was all.

Was it too early to leave? Yes, just hang out for a little while. There was time for one more pee before she left.

London

DCI Mike Lewis felt like there was a chainsaw in his head. Buzzing away relentlessly. Not even having a shower could shift it. Just one more drink, he had told Muriel. He should have listened to his own advice. But Muriel, bless her, hadn't nagged or demanded they leave. She had been at his side for a long time, and he appreciated her every day.

Like last night, when she'd taken photos in the pub. She had been an unofficial team member. She was always on his side, no matter what he did.

'Here's your coffee, love,' she said, coming into the living room.

'You're a sweetheart, you know that? My mother said I should keep you.'

'Your mother was a very wise woman.' She smiled at him. 'When you were in the shower, Sean Cargill called. He wants you to call him.'

'Okay. He's probably lying in bed with his head under the covers, trying to light his own farts again.' Holding on to the coffee mug and trying not to give himself a liquid vasectomy, he picked up the house phone from the side table and dialled the number from memory.

'Hello?' the man's voice at the other end said.

'You sound chipper this morning. Bloody madman.'

'Boss, listen. I was having the photos made up at the lab, so we could get a better look at this guy in the pub last night. And guess what?'

'I don't know.'

'Guess.'

'Christ, Sean, just fucking tell me.'

'Right. Get this: that twat Hogarth pointed to the man with the beard, right?'

'I believe he did, Sean.'

'Well, I had the photo blown up after Art put it into Photoshop and did his thing with it. There's another guy with a beard along from the one that Hogarth pointed to. Also reading a newspaper. I could see a tattoo on the inside of his right wrist.'

Lewis sipped the hot coffee. 'Don't keep me in suspense, lad.'

'It says, *Bark and Hair*.'

'You mean like Burke and Hare, those Scottish guys who murdered people and sold their bodies?' Lewis thought it was too early for this shit, even though it was gone midday.

'Almost. It's a play on words, boss,' Cargill said. 'It's like Burke and Hare, but it's *Bark* like a dog barks, and *Hair* like the hair on your head.'

'What the bloody hell does that mean?' Lewis asked.

'I looked it up. It's a crime podcast. Run by some arsehole called Ian Bark.'

'That name sounds familiar.'

'It should do; he's Leanne's ex-boyfriend.'

Lewis sat up, once again trying not to spill his coffee. 'He was in the pub last night?'

'He was. I thought that was a bit of an odd coincidence. So I went with Roy West this morning to the studio where this Bark geezer works, expecting it to be a home studio. It's not. It's in a little hotel. The landlady says he isn't there. He's away on holiday for a few days.'

'Where's he away to?' Lewis asked.

'Guess.'

'I'm not fucking guessing, Sean.'

'Scotland. To see his new girlfriend. Her name is Isla McGregor, apparently. And guess what she does for a living?'

'I swear to God, if you use that word one more time...'

'She's a detective, boss. First he was dating Leanne; now he's gone after another detective.'

'But maybe he's just using this Isla girl to get to Leanne.' Lewis put his coffee mug down. 'Good job, son. Now I need to make a phone call.'

TWENTY-THREE

Angie Fisher said she would follow Craig as she didn't know where the hell she was going. They went up the A911, through Crosshill, heading north at a fair clip.

'I've been to Scotland before, but never to this part,' Leanne said, doing the touristy thing by looking out of the window and pointing at sheep.

'You'll soon learn this off by heart,' Craig said. 'I got lost plenty of times when I came back up here to live and I was brought up here.'

Onto a B road, the 919, past the Balgedie Toll Tavern. Attached to a small fence outside the tavern were two traffic signs: left for the M90, right for Perth. Craig wished they were just going for a drive in the country so they could stop for a quick pie and chips and a couple of beers.

'I was thinking, now that you've been sent postcards and somebody calling himself The Traveller knows you're moving up here, you should move into my place. I have four bedrooms. Plenty of space. Plus, you still have to meet Finn, my German Shepherd.' He looked at her. 'You're not allergic to dogs, are you?'

She laughed. 'No. I love dogs.' She looked at him. 'What would Annie say about me moving into your house instead of her place?'

'I don't think Annie would have any problem with it. She was the one who offered you a place to stay right off the bat. She's practically living at my place just now, and we're on the verge of just making it official. Maybe she would like to move in as well. As long as you would be comfortable with that?'

'I'd love that. I really appreciate you not going mental when you found out I was transferring here.'

'Why would I go mental?' he asked.

She shrugged. 'It came out of the blue.'

Craig checked his mirror to make sure that Angie was still following him. She was.

'It was a pleasant surprise.' He quickly looked at Leanne. 'After what happened to Joe.'

'I couldn't believe it when you told me what happened to him. First Mum, then Joe.'

'His name is Chris Ward. The man who killed my son in the State Hospital. Joe had killed his wife in London.'

'Jesus.'

Further up the road, onto the A912. 'We're on the road that takes us past the hotel where the victims were found yesterday. The dead woman, Kathy. Not formally identified, but I'm convinced it's Richard Goode's dead wife.'

At the intersection where the hotel was, all signs of the previous day's police activity were gone. The metal fence panels had been linked again and the front door boarded up. Whatever forensic material there had been, it had already been taken. Had it been a normal house, Craig knew they would have still been there, but the place was in such bad shape that nothing else could be gathered.

'Over there,' Craig said.

Leanne looked over. 'Did the killer burn the place?'

Craig shook his head, indicated and took off, Angie right behind him. 'No. He started a fire and then put it out with a fire extinguisher. We can't figure out why he would do that. I mean, if it's the same guy who did the bodies in the nursing home in Glasgow, then he could have sent the place up. But he didn't. Two trains of thought. First, he heard the bus stop outside. You know the sound they make when their air brakes are put on? Maybe that alerted him. Or, maybe he just wanted to set a little fire, as that's his thing, but for some reason he didn't want to burn the hotel down. Maybe because it was already burnt.'

'It was control,' Leanne said, looking at Craig.

'I suppose it was.'

'No, really. I went on a course. We spent a week with a psychologist. Controlling a crime scene means he orchestrated every last thing. Burning the place he was in meant he was in control of every facet of the crime. Trust me, if he set that fire and put it out with an extinguisher, then that was a deliberate act. Not because he heard a bus stop. Because he wanted to see the flames. To control them.'

'That's a good theory, Leanne.'

'He knew the place.'

'We know the murder victim Richard Goode knew the place. He was a police officer but couldn't cut it on the force, so between jobs he worked in the kitchens in the hotel.'

'That must have been hard for him. Working a

job like that after being a police officer.' She looked at him. 'Did he know the manager? Of the hotel.'

'He knew the owner. What makes you ask?'

'Imagine Goode leaving the force and going to a hotel to ask for a menial job. And I don't mean that in a snobby way. I mean, he was in uniform, and now he wanted to scrub pots? It seems to me that he would have made a phone call to somebody he knew to ask for a job just to see him through for a bit. He wouldn't have been embarrassed or had to go cap in hand.'

'Makes sense. And we know he knew the owner, from his sister.'

'The killer knew him too. Knew his way around the place. He felt confident.'

Right onto the A913, Perth Road. A side road, just past the roundabout. A country road, going uphill. At the top, Craig stopped and could just see the ruined roof of the Campbells' house above the trees and the hedgerow that surrounded the property.

He got out, stretched his arms and legs, and yawned. Leanne got out the other side and stood looking at the old house. Angie pulled up behind them, and she and Max got out.

A cold, bitter wind came rushing around them, swaying the trees in the overgrown garden.

'Creepy-looking place,' Angie said. 'I bet it was nice in its day, though.'

'Aye, it looks solid enough. Not like the crap they build nowadays,' Craig said.

They walked closer to the house. Most of the roof was gone, a few blackened beams still clinging on for dear life. The windows were black eyes, unseeing now, any hint of a window frame long gone. There was no door in the main doorway.

'What was it Hopper said about Campbell again?' Max said.

'His family owned this house,' Leanne said. 'He came home one night and the place was well alight He tried to save his family and couldn't. His old man and other members of the family all died.'

Craig put his hands in his pockets and looked at the old building. 'Let me summarise then. Bruce Campbell's family dies in the fire. A young woman gets beaten by her boyfriend, two years ago. She dies, and gets brought back to Fife from Glasgow. Then somebody digs her up, and takes her corpse and her very-much-alive boyfriend to an abandoned nursing home, where he stabs the boyfriend to death. Then he sets the place on fire and lets it burn.' He turned to look at the others. 'If it's Bruce Campbell, why?'

They all stayed quiet.

'That's what's sticking with me,' Craig said, carrying on. 'Motive. Why now? Or two years ago, if we're assuming that Dennis Halloran was the first victim. Why wait all those years and start killing?'

'Unless he started in a different way, years earlier,' Leanne said.

'I had Max check through our system to see if there were any similar cases. That's how we hit on the Glasgow one. Max? You said Edinburgh had a similar one?'

'Yes, boss. I'm waiting for Harry McNeil to get back to me.'

'Chase him up. I want to know what that was all about.'

'I'll give him another call.' Max walked away from the house, taking his phone out.

Craig walked closer to the house, wondering exactly where the fire had started. And what caused it.

He walked back to the car. 'Leanne? First thing Monday morning, I'd like you to get a fire report from Scottish Fire and Rescue. I know things changed long after this fire, but they're bound to have records of this fire somewhere. Thirty years ago. If not, we'll have a talk with Hopper again. Meantime, let's go and talk to Bruce Campbell. See if we can jog his memory a bit. See what he remembers about the night of the fire. We can compare notes with the fire brigade.'

'Yes, sir.'

Max walked back to them. 'Harry sends his apologies to you, sir. One of the team was supposed to get back to you. Their murder case isn't really a murder case at all.'

They all stood looking at him, waiting for him to explain.

'They have an arson case that's ongoing. Somebody set fire to a house, and when it was put out, two bodies were found, but they weren't really bodies. They were mannequins. Both melted. But this is why it got flagged: one of them had a large knife sticking out of its chest.'

'How long ago was that?' Angie asked.

'Two and a half years ago, before the nursing home in Glasgow went on fire.'

'It sounds almost like it was a dry run,' Leanne said. 'And by doing it in Edinburgh and then Glasgow, he was hoping nothing would be linked.'

'Could be,' Max said.

'That would make sense. Does the dry run, then kills Halloran in Glasgow, and now Goode in Fife,' Craig said. 'I think it's time we went and spoke to Bruce Campbell. His place is still here in town, Max?'

The DI took his phone out and found the funeral director's business. 'Just along the road.'

'Let's go.'

TWENTY-FOUR

'Thanks for picking me up,' Ian Bark said to Isla. He smiled at her, his teeth shining through his thick beard. His hair was long and his eyebrows bushy. He looked a lot hairier in person than in his photos.

'No problem. I thought we could get a coffee.'

'I would love to, but can we do that later? I am so excited to be with you after we've been chatting for so long.'

'I am too.' She smiled at him.

'I'm going to take this podcast thing into outer space. I'm going to start doing a video version so it can go on YouTube. Then I can make money from that.' He turned to look at her. 'I'd like you on board.'

'It sounds exciting.' Isla smiled, thinking that

maybe it *was* time for a career change. 'What do you want to do first?'

He looked across at her like he was a small boy. 'Could we go and look at the hotel crime scene you were at yesterday?'

'How did you know about that?'

'It's been all over the news.' He smiled even more widely at her. 'I could get a feel for the place and it could be our first podcast together.'

'Okay. Let's go. It's about twenty minutes or so from here.'

She turned up the small road at the side of Dalgety Bay station and took off.

'How was your trip?' she asked Ian.

'Oh, you know, trains. Ever since deregulation, the train service has sucked.' He looked sideways at her. 'I did a podcast one time about a woman who was murdered on a train and left in the toilets.'

'Gruesome,' she said, but found that fascinating, from a detective's point of view.

They chatted more about true crime, Isla feeling comfortable in Bark's company, and a little while later, they arrived at the hotel. She parked off to the side in front of the abandoned chalets, which were boarded up and in disrepair.

Bark got out and looked at Isla. 'This is a real-life crime scene. I've been to a few, through some of my police sources, but this is my first in Scotland. And the crime hasn't even been solved.' He grinned at her. 'Imagine what it would be like filming this.'

'Pretty good, I would imagine. From a content creator's point of view.'

'You've got that right.' He opened the back door and reached in for his backpack.

Isla felt the cold wind bite into her as she locked her car. She wished she had put on a heavier jacket as they moved one of the metal fence panels and walked up the pathway to the front door.

It smelled of rot and damp and mould, but Bark loved it. 'What a great place!' He walked ahead of her, oblivious to the smell and the danger. 'Where were they found?'

'Upstairs. In one of the bedrooms.'

Bark laughed like a child. 'Let's go!' he shouted and took off, running up the stairs. Isla heard his feet thumping on the upper level as he ran out of sight.

'Please be careful, Ian!' she shouted, but all she could hear was laughter.

She tutted and hoped this wasn't going to go sideways. It was already a risk bringing him here. She could throw away her whole career. But then, hadn't she had doubts about staying on the force after Jessie decided to leave?

Jessie's moving to Glasgow, not leaving the force, a little voice in her head reminded her.

'Ian? You okay up there?'

No reply.

He was probably taking photos or videoing. She hoped he wasn't doing anything weird to himself up there. She carefully walked past the rubbish on the floor and started walking up the stairs. The smell was still bad up here, but there was some fresh air getting in through the dilapidated roof.

'Ian? Where are you?' she asked, but knew he would be in the room where the murder had taken place.

He wasn't.

'Ian? Stop messing about.'

She stood and listened, thinking that she'd heard something downstairs. Maybe the wind shifting stuff. She looked around the crime scene room again. Nothing. No sign of Ian. Now he was just playing fucking games, and starting to annoy her. Maybe coming here hadn't been such a good idea after all.

She left the room and looked across the hallway. That door was halfway closed. 'Ian? You in there?'

She stepped forward, looking along the dirty

hallway. Seeing nothing. Closer to the door. She gently pushed it, seeing nothing in the darkness beyond.

'Ian?'

She sensed something behind her, moving fast. Then darkness.

TWENTY-FIVE

The business was larger than Craig had envisaged. There was a public entrance at the front of the building, and the vehicles were parked in a large yard to the left.

They parked their cars and walked into the yard, where a young man was washing a hearse. An older man approached the building and looked at the four people standing there holding their warrant cards out.

'I wondered when you lot would be coming,' Bruce Campbell said.

'Mr Campbell?' Craig asked, not liking the aggression right off the bat.

'Aye. What about it?'

'We'd like to have a word, if we could.'

Campbell walked closer. 'Unless it's about buying a funeral plan, I'm not interested. If you could see yourselves out –'

'It's about Carla Hopper.'

Campbell looked at Craig. 'What about her?' Craig saw the colour leave the man's face.

'We're trying to find out who dug her up and took her back to Glasgow, where she was found in a fire,' Angie said, stepping forward and getting closer to the man.

'I have no idea what you're talking about.'

'Yes, you do. Don't fucking lie,' Angie said.

'First of all, I'm not lying. Yes, I was the undertaker who dealt with Carla, and second, I do not know who dug her up and took her to Glasgow. I'm never in Glasgow.' Campbell looked at Angie, like he wanted her to prove otherwise.

'We can have a warrant issued in five minutes,' she countered, ignoring the jibe about her city. 'We'll have so many uniforms crawling over this place, it'll look like a new fucking police station has been built here. Plus, we'll make a call to the local TV and radio stations and have photographers here. See how much business you get after that.'

'You wouldn't dare.'

'Imagine the headline: *local undertaker investi-*

gated for digging up a corpse and being involved in murder. That's just for starters. Think what the internet will do with that.'

Campbell drew in a deep breath and let it out slowly. 'Let's get out of the cold. Have a cup of coffee.'

He led the way into a working area in the back that smelled of chemicals and death. Craig was glad when Campbell took them through to a lounge area. He called somebody and asked the detectives to sit down. This room had couches and chairs, and it was somewhere a family could gather and think about their loved one.

A man brought through some coffees as they were settling. The room smelled a bit musty for Craig's liking, bringing back memories of his own father's funeral.

'I promise you there isn't any formaldehyde in the coffee,' Campbell said, sipping from the first mug.

The others grabbed a mug.

'Listen, I'm sorry I was so snappy,' Campbell said, sitting down. The others sat and listened. 'It was horrific for me. That poor girl. Some sick bastard dug her up, then took her away, and then murdered a man. A local man from here, no less! It's been a horrendous time. I lost work through it. They think I'm some kind of monster. I mean, not everybody, but word gets around.'

'You obviously heard about the bodies being found in the Gateway Hotel, just along the road,' Craig said.

'Same thing, isn't it? A woman already dead there, and that poor excuse for a man, Goode, murdered.'

'You didn't like Richard Goode, then?' Leanne said.

'He was one of you lot. A long time ago. Then he trained to be a nurse. Rumour had it, he was beating his wife. The bastard. I met him loads of times. I have the contract for the nursing home, so I'm there pretty regularly. I dealt with him a lot. Cocky bastard. I didn't like him and made no bones about it, and some say he got what he deserved.'

'We want to have a look at his wife's grave,' Craig said. 'The woman's body has an identifying mark on it.'

'A tattoo saying "I love Jesus",' Campbell said matter-of-factly.

'How did you know that?' Angie asked.

'I did her funeral. I saw the tattoo. It wasn't surrounded by neon flashing lights, but it wasn't exactly hidden either.' Campbell looked sombre for a moment. 'It's definitely her. Her grave's been tampered with. I had a look.'

'How do you know it's been tampered with?' Max asked.

'Well, there's a bloody great hole in the ground where she was buried and the coffin is there, open. As of half an hour ago. I went there after doing the funeral in Lochgelly. I wanted to have a look for myself. I wasn't sure the victim was Kathy, mind, but when Goode was mentioned on the radio, I just wanted a look. I would say it's his wife you found at the hotel.'

Craig looked at the others. 'We have two crime scenes, and the murder victims are both abusers. That's not a coincidence.'

'No, it's not,' Angie said.

Craig looked at Campbell again. 'What happened the night your family's house burned down? We've just been to have a look at it.'

Campbell drank some more coffee, and his mind took him somewhere else for a moment. Then he focused on Craig.

'My old man was a complete bastard. He knew his job alright, and he looked after his family. But sometimes, the drink got to him. He couldn't control it. It's what drove my mother away.'

'Your mother?' Max said. 'I thought she died in the fire as well?'

Campbell shook his head. 'That was my *step*mother. She was nice. She had a son, and she and my father had two more kids. They all died in the fire. Luckily, I had my best friend to help me. Sarah.'

'Robert Hopper told us you were good friends back then,' Craig said.

Campbell gave a short laugh. 'More than just good friends; she was my wife. We were married for ten years, but this business has me working all hours. Then she met Hopper again, the accountant, after many years. We split up, and she married him. He was one of our group too back then.'

'He didn't speak very highly of you,' Craig said.

'That doesn't surprise me,' Campbell replied. 'He hates me. You see, Carla was *my* daughter.'

'She had his name. Did he adopt her?' Max asked.

Campbell smiled. 'No. That was my little bit of *fuck you* to him. You see, Sarah and I kept in touch. We became better friends after we divorced. She would tell me about the problems she had with Hopper. I never liked him, not since the first time I clapped eyes on him when we were young adults. Sarah told me that they were trying for a child and it wasn't working. We ended up sleeping together, and hey presto! Miracle baby nine months later. We did a DNA test years later, and it confirmed Carla was mine. Now you see why I would never have dug her up, my own daughter. I was shattered by it all.

'Then one night after Carla was found in Glasgow, Sarah wanted to meet me in the cemetery. I turned up at the time we'd agreed, and I heard a scream. I had my car window open. I drove down to the grave and she wasn't there. Then I heard the scream again, just before the train came along. It was Sarah screaming, down by the tracks. I ran over, and I saw a car taking off from the side road on the other side of the tracks.'

'Did you see who was driving?' Leanne asked.

Campbell shook his head. 'No. I just saw a white car leaving at speed, and when it hit the main road, it went out of sight. I couldn't even tell you what make it was. I wanted to get out of there. I thought Sarah might have been kidnapped, but the train wouldn't have stopped for that. I've been to sites where a train has hit somebody. It stops. And that's what happened.'

'You think Hopper found out that Sarah was meeting you in the cemetery?' Angie asked.

'I'm not sure. He has a white car. That's the only link.'

'Do you think he could have dug up Carla?' Craig asked.

Campbell shook his head. 'No. A machine was used to dig her up. Hopper has trouble walking. I doubt he's physically capable of climbing into it. And before you ask, yes, I know how to use one. Just from watching the cemetery workers doing it. On the odd occasion. I mean, I'm not an expert, but when you watch what they're doing, you can pick up enough to use one.'

'Going back to the night of the fire at your house, where were you at the time?'

'Working. In the old building. The house and the business weren't in the same location back then. I was with other workers. I got a call from a neighbour telling me the house was on fire. Josh wasn't there either. He was away at the time.'

'Josh who?' Craig asked.

'Fraser. The minister. He's my stepbrother.'

TWENTY-SIX

'This is brilliant,' Ian Bark said. He stepped closer to Isla, who was standing on her tiptoes, her arms straight up above her, tied by a rope to a burnt beam. There was a gag in her mouth.

'Creating the best podcast that I've ever done.' He smiled at her. 'You see, I'll be able to describe to my listeners – and viewers! – how you and I visited the crime scene, and unknown to us, the killer was right here! Watching our every move. I had to fight him off. He ran, and I was wounded, but I managed to get you down from your position. Unfortunately, it was too late.'

Isla moved and mumbled behind the gag.

'I can't hear you. I'll slip the gag down, but if you

scream, I'll put it back in. Okay? Nod your head if you understand.'

Isla nodded.

Bark slipped the gag down. 'What do you want to say?'

'Fucking untie me right now and I might not boot you in the fucking baws!'

Bark laughed. 'You're a real spunky one. Just like Leanne. I actually dated her. I was just using her, of course. Her mother had been murdered, and she was vulnerable. I was going to do to her what I'm doing to you but she dumped me before I had the chance. Luckily, you responded to me when I wrote. I did a bit of research, and you were the only one who wrote back. I had bumped into Leanne one day and asked her if we could maybe get a coffee, and she refused. She told me she was moving to Scotland. So when I'm done with you, I'm going to take care of her.'

'You're a fucking weirdo.'

Bark laughed. 'I was expecting you to plead for your life.'

'Why should I? You're going to kill me anyway.'

'You could be nice to me. I could make it painless.'

Isla laughed. 'You're such a weasel. I would never beg for anything from you.'

'That's too bad.' He put the gag back in her mouth.

Isla heard the noise again, the same one she'd heard when she was in the other room.

So did Bark.

Too late.

TWENTY-SEVEN

The drive to Newburgh took five minutes. The church was small and unimposing. Angie stopped behind Craig again.

'Back-up is on the way,' he told her.

'Are we going to wait outside here?' Leanne asked.

'You are. You're not officially on duty until Monday. Max, stay outside with her. Angie and I are going in to talk to him.'

'No problem,' Leanne answered.

'I appreciate your input. Making that connection.'

'My mum was a bit religious. It rubbed off a bit,' she said.

Craig and Angie walked forward to the church

door. It opened easily and they stepped into the vestibule, and right away Craig could smell it.

Petrol.

They opened the door to the church proper, where the smell was much stronger.

'You shouldn't be here,' Major Josh Fraser said. He was standing holding a blowtorch. 'It's too dangerous. I've been storing the petrol up for when the time came. And that day is today. I knew it when I saw you' – he nodded to Angie – 'walking about the cemetery with the caretaker. I've poured sixteen gallons up here. It's burning my eyes to be honest. I was just making the final preparations, not expecting you to come by. What made you come here?'

'We were talking to your brother. Stepbrother. Bruce,' Craig said. 'He told us that Kathy had been married twice and you were her first love. My colleague figured out the tattoo: "I love Jesus". Jesus' name in Hebrew is *Yeshua*. Which translated into English is Joshua. You were all friends back then, weren't you, Josh? Except Robert Hopper wasn't the friendliest of blokes, was he?'

'He's a bastard. He didn't deserve her. Bruce went to meet Sarah in the cemetery that day. Did he tell you? He thinks that Hopper found out and chased Sarah right onto the train tracks. Killed her.

Bruce is wrong. It was me. I wasn't trying to hurt her. She suspected it was one of us who'd dug up Carla. She wanted to have it out with Bruce, because he's the one who knows how to operate the backhoe; she didn't know that I also know how. He told me she was meeting him, and I went a bit early. Sarah and I argued and she wouldn't listen. Then she started running and I chased her. The train was coming through as she ran blindly.'

'Why did you dig Carla and Kathy up?'

'When my mother married Campbell, Bruce and I became stepbrothers. My mother and his father started arguing all the time. I joined the army to get away from it. Somehow, a fire started and they all died in it. I wasn't there to save my mum. And I wasn't there to save Carla, or Kathy. Both were in abusive relationships. So I dug them up. I wanted them to watch as I took care of their abusers. I killed Dennis Halloran. Carla wasn't meant to get burnt, but she did.'

'Kathy?'

'I couldn't prove it, but I'm sure that bastard Goode killed her. Supposedly, he was in the nursing home at the time, but he could have slipped out and taken the dog from Kathy and shoved her in the river. She couldn't swim. Easy way to get rid of her.'

'What about the Edinburgh fire? With the mannequins?' Angie asked, the smell of the petrol nauseating.

'That was just a practice run. I wasn't going to kill innocent people.'

'Why don't you come outside with us?' Craig said. Then his phone rang. He ignored it.

'I can't do that. Answer your phone. Somebody might need you. Somebody needed me a long time ago, and I wasn't there for her.'

'Listen, Josh –' Craig started to say, but the minister had turned on the blowtorch and dropped it. A snake of fire started eating its way across the pulpit. Craig pushed Angie ahead of him, and they managed to get outside before the windows in the church were blown out, orange flames exploding out after them.

Max shoved Leanne behind the nearest car as the flames reached into the sky. Craig and Angie were racing across to them.

Then all hell let loose.

TWENTY-EIGHT

Craig's phone rang again. This time he answered it. 'I'm a bit busy, Annie. A church just exploded. I'll explain later. Got to go.'

'Isla's in trouble!' Annie screamed.

That got his attention. 'What do you mean?' he asked above the roar of the fire. They could hear sirens in the distance. Fire brigade, their own back-up. Probably ambulances too, though they wouldn't be needed.

'I'm in the car, heading up to the hotel we were at. The crime scene. She's in trouble, Jimmy!'

'How do you know she's in trouble?'

'I was upstairs in the kitchen when the Ring doorbell gave me a notification. I thought it might be Isla, so I went downstairs to answer it.'

'You should never answer it until you know who's there.'

'I know, I know. Fuck. There was a postcard through the letterbox. Delivered by somebody with a beard. Control has been trying to get hold of you. They called here. A message from Leanne's old boss, DCI Mike Lewis. To let you know there's a guy who has been following Leanne in London. I called him, explained who I was, and he sent me a photo of the guy with the beard. He has a tattoo on his wrist. It's Ian Bark, the man Isla picked up from the station. I think he's going to kill Isla. He was at our door! He put a postcard through the letterbox and then walked away. It was a tourist postcard. On the back it says, "Goodbye, Isla"!'

'Jesus. Where are you now?'

'Near the Gateway Hotel.'

'How do you know she's there?' Craig shouted as the sirens got closer.

'She has a tracker in her car. I made her give me the log-in for the app.'

'Her car's getting fixed.'

'It was finished early. She got her car this morning. I tracked her to the hotel.'

'I'm just along the road. How far away are you?'

'Two minutes.'

'Do not go in there until I get there! Do you understand?'

But the call had been cut off.

'Shite. Leanne! With me. Angie, you can come too if you like. I'll explain on the way. Max, can you handle things here? We need to get back to the crime scene at the hotel.'

'Go! I'll take care of it.'

The three detectives jumped into the car, and Craig took off, heading back along the main street, lights and sirens on.

He hoped he wasn't too late.

TWENTY-NINE

Isla's arms were screaming at her. Her muscles were taut, aching and starting to feel like they weren't attached to her body. Her back was stiff and her legs felt like they had been running for miles with the strain of standing on her tiptoes.

The pain was nothing compared to when she looked into the eyes of the man standing in front of her. She could see the evil there, feel his intent radiating off him like a boiler about to explode.

Looking into his eyes because he was wearing a balaclava. Lying past him was Ian Bark, the man who was going to kill her. He was dead. This new man had made sure of that. The necktie had been dropped around his neck and pulled tight, and no matter how hard Bark had fought, it had no effect.

'Right then, tell me your name,' Balaclava said.

Was there any point in fighting this? Had she been given a second chance, or was this guy just fucking with her before he ended her life?

'DS Isla McGregor, Police Scotland.'

'Well then, DS Isla McGregor of Police Scotland, you want to tell me why you're trussed up like a Christmas turkey?'

His accent was English, well-spoken.

'His name is Ian Bark, and he's a true-crime podcaster. He was going to kill me and make it look like some nutcase had done it, and he had come along and found me. Something like that.'

'How long have you known him?'

'A few months. Only online. I'd never met him before today.' She locked eyes with him again. 'Please answer me one question: are you going to kill me? Because I really have to pee.'

'That depends. Are you going to behave when I cut you down?'

'Of course.'

'Why do I think you're lying to me, Isla?'

'I'm not, honestly. My arms feel like they're made of concrete.'

They could hear sirens in the distance. The man brought out a hunting knife.

'Oh God,' Isla said.

Balaclava stepped forward, raised the knife and... cut the rope. He held on to Isla so she wouldn't fall. He cut the rope off her wrists.

'Does anybody know you're here?'

'Not that I know of.'

'Don't lie to me, Isla. I can hear sirens. Are they coming here?'

'I have a tracker in my car. If somebody's looking for me, they'll know I'm here from that.'

'Good girl. Now, I want you to give a message to DCI Craig.' He reached into his back pocket, took out a postcard and showed her the image on the front. 'That man there' – he gestured to Ian Bark – 'has been sending postcards to Craig's daughter, Leanne. I sent her one, and she must have told him, and I think he sent her more, trying to scare her and hoping she would think it was me. That was naughty. I'm going to leave this card here for Leanne. And my message to Craig is: I'll see you again. My name? He doesn't know it. He only knows me as Chris Ward. He'll know that name for sure.'

He put the postcard on the floor. It showed a London bus.

'Take care, Isla. You never know, we might meet again. If you're there when I come back to kill him.'

And with that, Chris Ward left the room.

THIRTY

'Don't you do that to me again, girl,' Annie said, as Isla was being checked out in the back of an ambulance.

'I have the worst luck.'

'I'd say you had good luck this time,' Craig said. 'You're lucky to be alive.'

They were waiting to hear what had happened. The forensics team was back, going through the bedroom for the second time.

Stan Mackay came out of the hotel, holding up two evidence bags. One of them held the postcard. The other held a small camera.

'This was in the room. It has a SIM card. It looks like it was recording.'

'Can I read the postcard?' Craig asked.

Angie and Leanne were standing near the ambulance, just in case the fruitcake had decided to stay behind.

Mackay handed it over and Craig read it through the plastic: *Hello, Jimmy. Intel probably told you that I left for New York. I did. Then I got bored and decided to come back. I hope Leanne enjoys her new job. The Traveller.* There was a little drawing of a suitcase.

'He said you would know him as Chris Ward,' Isla said. 'He had an English accent, and I couldn't see what he looked like. Just his cold blue eyes.'

Her words shot ice through Craig as he handed the bag back.

I don't know where he'll be. We'll have to stay vigilant. Leanne? It's not too late for you to go somewhere else. Somewhere safe.'

'I'm not running away from him. I'm here to stay.'

'I'm just through in Glasgow if you need me,' Angie said.

'Thanks, Angie,' Leanne said, and gave her a hug.

'And I'll be around in your life, big time,' Annie said.

'Thanks, Annie.'

'And obviously, when I'm not on a stretcher, I'll be your wing-woman,' Isla said.

'Thanks, Isla. I appreciate it.' Leanne looked at her father. 'I want to make my dad proud. And I can't do that if I run back to London. I'm here for the long haul.'

Craig hugged his daughter, holding on to her. Chris Ward was not going to win this battle.

THIRTY-ONE

Monday

It was her first official day in the office, and Leanne had been whisked away to see DCS Bill Walker, who wanted to give her a pep talk. And probably tell her what a bastard her father was, Craig thought. Now she was back, standing at the whiteboard.

Craig had called his ex-wife and told her about Chris Ward. She'd had an affair with the man when she was living near the hospital. She was indifferent.

'Leanne's first day,' Craig said, 'and we sat down and looked at the video that forensics took from the SIM card. Bark had placed the camera there and recorded tying Isla to the roof beam. Then the masked man killed him with a necktie. That exonerates Isla. She's on administrative leave but will probably be back next week. Anybody got any questions?'

DS Gary Menzies shot his hand up. 'Do you think you're my real dad as well?'

Craig shook his head. 'Definitely not.'

They all laughed.

'Right, to get back to our case: the Reverend Joshua Fraser was found in the church, burnt to a crisp. He felt guilty about leaving his mother behind in an abusive relationship when he went to join the army. His mother died in a fire. Fraser's friend's daughter and a woman he had loved years earlier were both in abusive relationships. He dug them up after they were killed by their partners; he wanted their killers to see them one last time before he killed them. Then he would read the eulogy at their second funerals when they were reburied. In his mind, he was giving the women a chance to watch their attackers get what they deserved, in Fraser's eyes.'

Max spoke up. 'We think he had these feelings when he was in the army, but it wasn't until a few years ago, after he retired from the army, that he acted on them.'

'Sarah Hopper's death was his fault,' Craig said. 'She went to the cemetery to have it out with Bruce

Campbell, about to accuse him of digging up Carla, but Fraser went, and she ran from him, and he couldn't catch her. He just wanted to explain, but she ran in front of a train. He was devastated about that.'

'And then we had the podcaster take Isla. It was a fun weekend,' Max said.

'At least Bruce Campbell gets the job of driving Bark back down to London. And as we know, each county demands a fee as the hearse passes through it. So he'll make a few notes doing that.'

'Do you think Bark killed other people?' Gary asked.

'Isla said not. He told her she was going to be the first victim. But who knows? Now, I just want to say one final thing,' Craig said. 'Although Leanne is my daughter, in here she's just another team member. No special favours. Just playing by the rule book. And talking of which, I think she should celebrate by doing a doughnut run to Greggs. Gary? You can drive her. Show her where she's going...'

THIRTY-TWO

Later that evening, with Finn lying at Leanne's feet as they watched TV, Craig felt good. Leanne had moved in until she found her own place. Annie had moved in as well. They were all one big, happy family. Not a care in the world.

Outside Craig's house, a man walked by. If Craig had looked out of his window, he wouldn't have had any cause for concern. The man was carrying a small suitcase.

'I have to leave now, Jim,' Chris Ward said. 'But we'll meet again one day.'

AFTERWORD

I would like to take this opportunity to thank a few people who helped on this journey.

First of all, Steven Mitchell, British Army, for his advice regarding chaplains in the army. Secondly, Leanne Chalmers, for allowing me to use her name in this book and subsequent Craig novels. If you're ever up in the Perth region of Scotland, I'd recommend a visit to the Touchdown café at Perth Airport in Scone, owned by Leanne's mum.

Thanks also to my wife Debbie, and to my daughter Sam, who is, as always, my sounding board on the dog walk, letting me bounce ideas off her. To Jacqueline, as usual, who has a superpower that not even a Marvel character can compete with. And to

AFTERWORD

my two dogs, Bear and Bella, who are asleep under my desk as I write this.

And most importantly, to you, the reader. With all my gratitude.

If anybody wants to get in touch, please feel free to contact me through the contact button on my website.

www.johncarsonauthor.com

Until next time, stay safe my friends.

John Carson
New York
January 2025

ABOUT THE AUTHOR

John Carson is originally from Edinburgh, Scotland, but now lives with his wife and family in New York State. And two dogs. And four cats.

www.johncarsonauthor.com

Printed in Great Britain
by Amazon